SALVAGE TITLE

BOOK ONE OF THE
SALVAGE TITLE TRILOGY

Kevin Steverson

Theogony Books
Virginia Beach, VA

Chris Kennedy/Theogony Books
2052 Bierce Dr.
Virginia Beach, VA 23454
http://chriskennedypublishing.com/

Publisher's Note: This is a work of fiction. Names, characters, places, and incidents are a product of the author's imagination. Locales and public names are sometimes used for atmospheric purposes. Any resemblance to actual people, living or dead, or to businesses, companies, events, institutions, or locales is completely coincidental.

Ordering Information:
Quantity sales. Special discounts are available on quantity purchases by corporations, associations, and others. For details, contact the "Special Sales Department" at the address above.

Salvage Title/Kevin Steverson. -- 1st ed.
ISBN 978-1948485593

Acknowledgements

First, I would like to thank the good Lord above for everything...literally, everything.

I want to thank my wife, Stacey, for encouraging me to just write the story and allowing me to talk things through with her. I realize now that she never really gave me an opinion, she just listened, and it helped immensely.

A grateful thank you goes out to my publisher Chris Kennedy. He took a chance on me and I'll never forget it.

Thanks to the guys in Cypress Spring for their friendship and support. Chasing dreams is no easy task, something they know full well.

I can't forget the guys that read my writing first, Mike and Dustin. Some things they read for me will never see the light of day. Thanks guys.

Finally, I would like to dedicate this book to my Mother and Father. She was an avid science fiction fan. And I'm sure she read it over my shoulder as I typed. I followed my Father's footsteps into the Army, I know he would have liked the military aspects of the story.

Chapter One

Four tons of steel and armor plating hung in the air, swaying slightly from the sudden stop of the grappler's claws. Harmon Tomeral wiped the sweat off his brow before it could run down into his eyes. *It was a hot one out there...again*, he thought. He was inside an eighty-ton machine with cool air blowing full blast, and he still felt the heat from outside.

The machine's official name was the Scrap Mover 80 XL. Everybody who worked at Rinto's Scrap Yard just called it the Grappler. It was a cross between a battle tank, an excavator, and a mech. Its base was like a tank, sitting on huge tracks with a humanoid-shaped cockpit on top. In addition to the blade up front there were two "arms" that extended out of the body, which each ended in four-fingered claws.

Harmon had been moving scrap from the giant pile in front of the conveyer to the belt that brought it into the furnace building. Once there, it was melted down, separated, and processed into half-ton blocks to be shipped to the factories here on Joth, as well as off-planet to various shipbuilding sites and factories.

It was a profitable business for Rinto. Scrap from sections of ships, battle stations, spaceports, tanks, armored personnel carriers, and even old mechs were melted down to become material for more of the same. Most of the time, it came down to the planet having already been cut into manageable chunks. Once salvagers claimed rights on anything they couldn't sell whole, they cut it up with lasers, loaded it into haulers, and brought it down to Rinto. He was the only game in town, since Rinto's was the only recycler on the planet that dealt in it.

It was junk. For the most part, anything truly valuable found by the salvagers was kept on their ship to be sold on other, more advanced planets in other systems, not on a planet like Joth. The system had a shipbuilding industry, sure, but everything needed to build spacecraft was fabricated on Tretra, the other inhabited planet in the system. The parts were then sent out to the shipyards in orbit around Tretra.

That planet. Harmon hated that planet. It was nothing like Joth. It was all blues and greens, puffy white clouds, beautiful beaches, and mountains. It was so picture perfect it made him sick. Harmon knew better.

It was also where the Tretrayon System Academy was located. The academy where he graduated from the Officer Training Program in the top ten percent. The top fifteen percent were *supposed* to be guaranteed an active commissioned slot into the Tretrayon Defensive Fleet. Only that didn't happen; politics happened. He wasn't from Tretra. He was from the planet Joth and was attending on a warball scholarship. It was all well and good when he led the team to the System School Championship three years in a row—but to let him actively serve in the System Defense Fleet as an officer just wasn't going to happen. Politics.

Harmon shook his head and pulled himself from the memory. The grappler's arms swung the load of scrap metal to the wide belt, and Harmon spun the body back around and reached for more. The machine moved with precision and, on occasion just to see if he could, he would pick up small pieces with the huge claws to maintain his delicate touch on the controls. The work Clip had done to its servos, programming, and guidance made them seem like part of him, and it was nothing short of genius.

He called Clip on the Grappler's comms unit. "Hey Clip."

"Hey man, what's up?" Clip's voice sounded hollow, as if he was inside something.

"I haven't found anything useful today. No motors, servos, or power cells are in this new load. I thought for sure I would find something. The Wren said he brought it in from outside the system, but today has officially sucked for our project. Do you think Rinto would let us have some of the good stuff from the warehouse?" Harmon asked.

"I can ask, but I doubt it. He doesn't mind us taking a little something here or there as long as it isn't too valuable. You know he likes to make those credits where he can." Clip sounded a little clearer.

Whatever he was working on, he was outside of it now. Harmon looked at the time display. "Well, it'll be quitting time here in about thirty minutes; I was hoping to find the power cell we need to test it. If I don't find anything today, we'll have to try next weekend."

"Alright, man…owww!" Harmon heard a sizzle and pop as Clip answered, and he smiled.

Clip Kolget was a great computer tech and programmer but was only a fair mechanic and electrician. He could take apart and repair or build just about anything. All he needed was the material and some time. The material didn't have to be exactly right, either. He could adapt, rewire, and reprogram most things to get the desired results. Well, close to what you needed anyway, even if he did get shocked. A lot.

Harmon and Clip were friends but acted more like brothers. They had grown up together in "the system." Their entire town had been destroyed when it was covered in a freak sandstorm when they were eight years old. The news vids had called it the storm of the century. There had only been fourteen survivors when the rescue teams had finally dug down to the elementary school basement. It was the only structure still somewhat intact after the storm swept in from the Great Middle Desert.

In reality, the whole planet was a desert. In the winter, it only got down to the low nineties at the poles. On days like today, it could reach one hundred and twenty degrees Fahrenheit in the shade. Their town wasn't the only one to get swallowed up in that storm, and a lot of children had been brought to the city from the wastelands.

Moving the grappler forward, Harmon decided to drop one more load onto the conveyer belt and call it quits for the week. The arms reached out, and the claws dug in, but a warning light flashed yellow twice. Something had stopped the claw on the right arm from closing. *Great. Now I have to get out in this heat.* He really didn't mind doing it, though. It happened several times a week, and sometimes he found items they needed. He just wished it had happened earlier in the day.

Before he opened the cockpit of the machine, he scraped away all the junk he could from where the claw had been caught. He could see there was a twelve-by-twelve container still connected to a piece of bulkhead. It looked like a sealed room from a corvette, the kind of ship he had trained on for two summers while at the academy. He could see the access panel on the front of the container. He had no idea how this could have gotten past the salvage company when they were cutting the ship into sections. Their screw-up was his good luck.

He made a call to Clip, then cracked the cockpit seal on the grappler. Immediately, he felt the heat pour into the pilot area. He didn't care, though; there might be something they needed inside the vault. He could hope, anyway.

He was standing in front of the container when Clip floated up in an ancient hovercraft that was far past its usefulness anywhere outside of Rinto's property. Its motor rattled and blew a little smoke, but it was fine for getting around the thousand-acre junkyard. Clip left it running and hopped off the low-hanging side. It was about a foot closer to the ground. Clip could fix it, of course; he just hadn't gotten around to it. His days were filled with repairing equipment and machinery that helped Rinto turn a profit.

"Alright, what do we have here?" He clapped and rubbed his hands together. Harmon noticed that one of his glove fingers had a hole and a scorch mark on the back of it.

Clip reached into the hovercraft and grabbed his kit. It was a backpack full of tools, small lasers, diagnostic equipment, some small power cells, and his sound box.

The sound box was his own creation—he had been reading about antique technology again. The iPod had been invented thousands of years before, back on Earth; he thought it was cool to have something dedicated solely to music and nothing else. Clip had made his own version with an external speaker as well as the ability to link to his earpiece. Sure, he could listen to music from his slate via the Galactic Net, but unless he was connected to the net, the slate was limited to what he had previously downloaded. It couldn't hold all the music that his sound box held, either. He said the sound box held *all* the music.

Clip liked to tell anyone who cared to listen that he not only had all of Earth's music, but also everything put out in all of the human systems as well. It also held a lot of music other races had created. Harmon didn't believe it. Sure, it held a lot of music, but there were thousands of known races. There was no way it had that kind of storage.

Harmon stood back as Clip went to work on the access panel. Music was blaring from the box, and Harmon recognized it. *Bootleg Style* by Cypress Spring from the twenty-first century. Nice choice.

The classics were still the classics. He wondered what a *southern girl* was, compared to the other girls on Earth back then. Clip would probably know.

The first thing Clip did was get power to the door and the access panel. Two of his power cells did the trick once he had them wired to the container. He then pulled out his slate and connected it. It lit up, and his fingers flew across it. It took him a few minutes to establish a link, then he programmed it to search for the combination to the access panel.

"Is it from a human ship?" Harmon asked, curious.

"I don't think so, but it doesn't matter; ones and zeros are still ones and zeros when it comes to computers. It's universal. I mean, there are some things you have to know to get other races' computers to run right, but it's not that hard," Clip said.

Harmon shook his head. *Riiigghht,* he thought. He knew better. Clip's intelligence test results were completely off the charts. Clip opted to go to work at Rinto's right after secondary school because there was nothing for him to learn at the colleges and universities on either Tretra or Joth. He could have received academic scholarships for advanced degrees on a number of nearby systems. He could have even gone all the way to Earth and attended the University of Georgia if he wanted. The problem was getting there. The schools would have provided free tuition if he could just have paid to get there.

Secondary school had been rough on Clip. He was a small guy that made excellent grades without trying. It would have been worse if Harmon hadn't let everyone know that Clip was his brother. They lived in the same foster center, so it was mostly true. The first day of school, Harmon had laid down the law—if you messed with Clip, you messed up.

At the age of fourteen, he beat three seniors senseless for attempting to put Clip in a trash container. One of them was a Yalteen, a member of a race of large humanoids from two systems over. It wasn't a fair fight—they should have brought more people with them. Harmon hated bullies.

After the suspension ended, the school's Warball coach came to see him. He started that season as a freshman and worked on using it to earn a scholarship to the academy. By the time he graduated, he was six feet two inches with two hundred and twenty pounds of muscle. He got the scholarship and a shot at going into space. It was the longest time he'd ever spent away from his foster brother, but he couldn't turn it down.

Clip stayed on Joth and went to work for Rinto. He figured it was a job that would get him access to all kinds of technical stuff, servos, motors, and maybe even some alien computers. The first week he was there, he tweaked the equipment and increased the plant's recycled steel production by 12 percent. Rinto was eternally grateful, as it put him solidly into the profit column instead of toeing the line between profit and loss. When Harmon came back to the planet after the academy, Rinto hired him on the spot on Clip's recommendation. After he saw Harmon operate the grappler and got to know him, he was glad he did.

A steady beeping brought Harmon back to the present. Clip's program had succeeded in unlocking the container. "Right on!" Clip exclaimed. He was always using expressions hundreds or more years out of style. "Let's see what we have; I hope this one isn't empty, too." Last month they'd come across a smaller vault, but it had been empty.

Harmon stepped up and wedged his hands into the small opening the door had made when it disengaged the locks. There wasn't enough power in the small cells Clip used to open it any further. He put his weight into it, and the door opened enough for them to get inside. Before they went in, Harmon placed a piece of pipe in the doorway so it couldn't close and lock on them, baking them alive before anyone realized they were missing.

Daylight shone in through the doorway, and they both froze in place; the weapons vault was full. In it were two racks of rifles, stacked on top of each other. One held twenty magnetic kinetic rifles, and the other held some type of laser rifle. There was a rack of pistols of various types. There were three cases of flechette grenades and one of thermite. There were cases of ammunition and power clips for the rifles and pistols, and all the weapons looked to be in good shape, even if they were of a strange design and clearly not made in this system. Harmon couldn't tell what system they had been made in, but he could tell what they were.

There were three upright containers on one side and three more against the back wall that looked like lockers. Five of the containers were not locked, so Clip opened them. The first three each held two sets of light battle armor that looked like it was designed for a humanoid race with four arms. The helmets looked like the ones Harmon had worn at the academy, but they were a little long in the face. The next container held a heavy battle suit—one that could be sealed against vacuum. It was also designed for a being with four arms. All the armor showed signs of wear, with scuffed helmets. The fifth container held shelves with three sizes of power cells on them. The largest power cells—four of them—were big enough to run a mech.

Harmon tried to force the handle open on the last container, thinking it may have gotten stuck over time, but it was locked and all he did was hurt his hand. The vault seemed like it had been closed for years.

Clip laughed and said, "That won't work. It's not age or metal fatigue keeping the door closed. Look at this stuff. It may be old, but it has been sealed in for years. It's all in great shape."

"Well, work some of your tech magic then, 'Puter Boy," Harmon said, shaking out his hand.

Clip pulled out a small laser pen and went to work on the container. It took another ten minutes, but finally he was through to the locking mechanism. It didn't take long after that to get it open.

Inside, there were two items—an eight-inch cube on a shelf that looked like a hard drive or a computer and the large power cell it was connected to. Harmon reached for it, but Clip grabbed his arm.

"Don't! Let me check it before you move it. It's hooked up to that power cell for a reason. I want to know why."

Harmon shrugged. "Okay, but I don't see any lights; it has probably been dead for years."

Clip took a sensor reader out of his kit, one of the many tools he had improved. He checked the cell and the device. There was a faint amount of power running to it that barely registered on his screen. There were several ports on the back along with the slot where the power cell was hooked in. He checked to make sure the connections were tight, he then carried the two devices to the hovercraft.

Clip then called Rinto's personal comm from the communicator in the hovercraft. When Rinto answered, Clip looked at Harmon and winked. "Hey boss, we found some stuff worth a hovercraft full of credit...probably two. Can we have it?" he asked.

Rinto had left for the day, right after lunch. It was the last day of the week, and he liked to go to the track and watch the chinto races. He laughed at Clip. "*Yeah, sure you did. Can you power up that little project you guys have been putting together with it?*"

"Well, yeah, I might be able to figure it out and use it," said Clip. "Maybe."

"I tell you what, you can have whatever you found, but if you get that thing running, I want to be there when you enter it," Rinto said.

"Deal!" Harmon said over Clip's shoulder.

Harmon didn't feel too bad about taking all the gear they found. Clip *had* called Rinto and told him they found some valuable stuff. It wasn't their fault if he didn't believe them. It was getting dark, though not noticeably cooler, as they started loading up everything they'd found. It took them two hours and three trips to get everything to their place on the other side of the city using Clip's small personal hovercraft and the yard's ancient hovercraft. It was a good thing they didn't get stopped by the authorities. Not because of the weapons—on Joth, everyone had the right to own weapons—but because of the yard's hovercraft. It wasn't registered.

* * * * *

Chapter Two

They lived in an old warehouse near the Star Port in Purlit, the largest city on the planet. The population of the city was around one million. It was located on the northern part of the planet near the pole.

The entire planet only had thirty million sentient beings on it. Most lived near the poles, where it was the coolest. The area near the equator on Joth never dropped below one hundred and forty degrees, even at night. During the daylight hours it reached upward of two hundred.

The city was comprised of humans and many other races, but mostly humans. They were settlers and descendants of settlers from Tretra, the next planet closer to the system's star, Tretrayon.

Tretrayon shone down mercilessly onto Joth. The system had fourteen planets, and Joth was the second planet from its star. The next planet was Tretra. Tretrayon was a star similar in size and rating to Sol, back in the home world system, and Tretra was the most Earth-like planet in the system. Its gravity was just ten percent more than Earth's, and it had a twenty-five-hour day. It had been the planet originally colonized thousands of years ago.

Both planets had atmospheres suitable for humans, but Joth had not been initially colonized because of its extreme temperatures. It also had a gravity just a little more than its sister planet, and, though its rotation was a little longer, the whole system went by the same twenty-five-hour time schedule. There were no oceans to speak of on Joth. There were several large lakes near the poles, but they were not enough to provide water for the entire planet.

Out of necessity, the atmosphere moisture collection industry on Joth was considered one of the best in their region of the galaxy. Though it was hot, settlers had come for one reason or another. Life could be hard on the planet Joth, and its residents took pride in that fact.

Of the dozens of different races living on Joth, the Prithmar made up the next largest population after humans, with over ten million. They had settled on Joth as refugees over eight hundred years prior, after their home world had been decimated in a multi-system war. The planet's environment was close to their home world, with the same average temperature and atmospheric moisture content. The Prithmar were the primary reason for the moisture collection industry advancement—it had been a way of life on their home planet.

Harmon and Clip rented the warehouse from the Farnog Corporation, one of the companies involved in the moisture collection business. It was Prithmar-owned, though it employed all races. Harmon and Clip had run across the opportunity about eight months ago, when Zerith, a friend from secondary school, let them know his parent's business had outgrown it. It was perfect for their plan.

Zerith's parent had converted one end of the warehouse to a large three-bedroom apartment, which worked out well for the three friends. For Clip and Harmon, having a Prithmar as a roommate was no different than having anybody else. On Joth, very few were xenophobic; the planet had such a diverse population for so long, it was just something that didn't exist. The same couldn't be said for the rest of the galaxy. It couldn't even be said about their sister planet Tretra.

* * *

Zerith came home from his job as a fusion plant technician at the family business shortly after they had closed the warehouse bay door. He came through the apartment and out into the bay. It was a room about the size of a warball field, with a roof fifty feet above.

Zerith was a little shorter than Clip—only about five-foot-tall and slender—as was most of his reptilian race. His small scales were a dusty bronze color, which were a bit lighter in his face. His tail extended about two feet behind him through a slot in his clothes. The end was slowly twitching, as he watched Harmon refill the last locker. He scratched the side of his head with one of the three fingers on his hand and ate a piece of fruit while trying to figure out what the weapons and ammunition were doing in their warehouse.

"What iss all thiss?" he asked, the slight stretching of some of his consonants barely noticeable. Over the years, his race had learned to speak Earth Common.

For the most part, a translator wasn't needed. They each had one, but it was for speaking to some of the other races in their city. Most beings had one programmed into their personal comps and linked in to an earpiece. The ones used on Joth had all the languages in the system programmed into them as well as a few from nearby systems. If one could afford it, there were translation programs that had *all* the known languages. The three of them couldn't afford one. Zerith's family had credits, but it was tradition for a Prithmar to earn their own way through life. There were no handouts, and any type of inheritance went right back into the family businesses.

"This is the mother lode, that's what it is," said Harmon.

"Can you usse thesse weaponss in the mech?" Zerith asked, looking over toward the corner of the room at a huge war machine that was partially assembled.

"Well, we can't use any of the weapons, but the power cells were just what we needed to put it together and test it," Clip said, clearly excited.

"Then, we can usse them in the ssecond phasse of the plan, for protecting what we claim," Zerith stated, as if the first part were going to go as planned.

"Exactly! I'm going to win this thing," Harmon said.

Harmon walked over and looked at the mech. It was...well, it was a sight to see. Clip and Zerith had built it from parts of damaged war machines that had come through the scrapyard. Harmon had helped with labor. Some pieces were of human design, and others were from machines other races used. Most of it was old. There were parts from outdated mechs and parts that Clip had made work, though they clearly did not belong.

The legs were from a mech that had first come off an assembly line two hundred years ago.

The main part of the body was of a design they still couldn't identify. It had been brought in by Yarkle, a Wend that came into the system a couple times a year to sell to Rinto. He mostly brought ship parts, but occasionally he had war machines, or what was left of them. The last load Harmon had been working through had been brought in by Yarkle.

The arms were Clip's design. They resembled a modern mech's arms. But the way they were manipulated by the pilot was almost human-like. Well, it would be, Clip had said. They had yet to power the machine up. They would find out that weekend. All three of them knew they wouldn't get much sleep. There was too much to do, too much at stake.

Forty-eight hours later, they sat on a table drinking the last of their celebratory beer. Zerith drank a much stronger Prithmar brand; his digestive system could handle the extra alcohol. They all had slept a few hours the night before, but not too many.

The mech was ready to be tested. They had connected all of the parts and put two power cells into the machine. One would have worked and powered the mech for more than a day's use.

Over the last few months, Clip and Zerith had completely re-wired the entire war machine and pieced together an operating system. Instead of one small computer to run the machine, it had several. It was as ugly as anything Harmon had ever seen, but he trusted Clip. If Clip said it was going to work, then it would work. It may need adjusting, but it would work. He needed it to work.

Their plan was for Harmon to enter the Top Fleet Marine competition next month. The Tretrayon Defense Fleet held the competition every year. This year it was scheduled to be on Joth.

The type of competition changed every year. The scenario this year was based on planet operations. Dropping in from high altitude, movement to a target, and other various tasks that had to be performed at the target. After the mech operations, there were several tasks that each Marine had to perform. It was open to the entire fleet. A Marine would use their assigned mech in it, receiving scores on a point system, for all the tasks.

The prize was one hundred thousand credits. Every year, Marines went through unit level competitions to become the top Marine in their unit so they could compete for the annual prize and prestige. Winning the competition meant that they were guaranteed fast track promotions, and, with shrewd investments, a comfortable life after their fleet time was up.

For Harmon and the guys, the prize money was more than enough to put a down payment on a used ship and book a ride on a merchant ship leaving their system through the gate—smaller ships could piggy back onto larger ships for a fee, and they planned to become salvagers. That's where the real credits were—selling pieces of ships from past wars.

"I'm ready, let's do this." Harmon said.

"OK, just remember, I may have to make some programming adjustments," Clip said.

"Thiss iss exciting," Zerith said, his tail waving at the tip. He crunched and chewed the seed of the fruit he had been eating.

Harmon climbed up the right leg and eased backward into the mech. He plugged in the leads on his helmet and slid his arms into their slots in the upper chest. He initiated start-up and closed the canopy. Before the canopy closed and sealed, the screens came on.

Inside the mech, he could see what was around him through the cameras mounted in the body of the mech. He had three screens enabling him to look in three different directions: forward, left, and right. As he turned his head, the screens panned, giving him the illusion the mech had a head, and it turned. There was also a camera with which he could see behind him, if he chose.

Harmon tested the communications first. "How does it sound?" he asked.

"Sounds good out here, man," Clip answered back from his personal comm.

"Sounds good in here, too, though I should probably have put in earpieces. Or get a better helmet. It's pretty loud in here when it's running," he said.

"Gotcha. Zee says he can get that set up for you. His company has some for workers in the plant. There's going to be several things we need to work on in the next few weeks," Clip responded.

"Visuals are good. All the lights are in the green. I am going to step forward. Stay back," Harmon said. He picked his left foot up and began walking forward. It felt right. Clip had used the same movement designs that were in modern mechs. Harmon had spent plenty of time in a mech while at the academy, as he had been aiming for a commissioned slot in the Tretrayon Defense Fleet's Marine Corps. Four years of training, including his summer breaks, had been for nothing. Until now, that is.

When Harmon slid into the cockpit, he had inserted his feet into the "boots." These were fitted slots for his feet in the upper thighs of the machine. As he lifted his feet to walk normally inside the machine, its limbs mimicked his movements. He could pivot on his feet and the machine would do the same. He could jump, and, depending on how much effort he put in to it, the mech would perform the same action with small jumps or large jumps. Harmon moved around in the warehouse, getting used to being in a mech again. The grappler at work was similar, and he had spent thousands of hours in it. It was on tracks, though, and not quite the same.

He couldn't test the weapons on the mech because they didn't have the ammunition. There was a magnetic rail gun on the right arm and a slot on both shoulders for a missile rack. There was also a compartment on the left thigh for one of the grenade rifles that were issued to mech pilots in the Corps, but they had no rifle.

Zerith knew someone that worked in the rail gun plant, and she had provided the parts to the railgun over a month ago. It had been easy for her to get the parts out. There was no over-the-top security in the plant. After all, why would someone need parts to a railgun that only worked on a mech? Who had mechs but the military? The manufacturing plant belonged to her family, and she was happy to gift them to Zerith.

They had been working on the machine for the last six months. Harmon didn't want to know where Clip got the arming and aiming program for the weapons, but the aiming reticle popped into view when he initiated it, so it worked. He suspected Clip wrote the programming himself. As for the parts, you never knew with Zerith around; he knew beings everywhere. Zerith could get his little hands on all kinds of parts and pieces they couldn't find in the scrapyard.

Harmon hit the foot thrusters with just a tap. They fired off and lifted the mech to about twenty feet up. When he came back down and landed, he bent his knees, absorbing the shock. It didn't cause any damage to the machine; no warning lights came on. Harmon did, however, feel it in his own knees and hips, and it jarred him. *Should have used the thrusters to slow myself down,* he thought. He was a little rusty, like the outside of the mech.

Zerith turned the lights out in the warehouse. Harmon switched over to infra-red and saw darkness—and nothing else. He couldn't see a thing. Zerith turned the lights back on. He popped the cockpit, and Zerith and Clip climbed up a leg to see if they could figure it out. Zerith finally traced it. A relay had come loose due to his hard landing. Zerith killed the lights again, and this time it worked.

Over the next two weeks, they tinkered with the mech every night and on the weekends, tightening loose wiring and relays. When Clip was working on programming and Zerith was tinkering with the legs, Harmon would work out in the far corner of the bay with weights and the hanging bag. He also ran every night through the neighborhood.

Zerith secured some paint. It was the same dark grey paint used on the Corps' mechs. He even painted "Lieutenant Tomeral" on a nameplate on the upper body of the mech.

Harmon was a Lieutenant in the Inactive Reserves of the Tretrayon Defense Fleet Marine Corps. He had not been selected to go into the fleet, but since he didn't resign his commission, he was in the Inactive Reserves. It was the only thing he got out of the academy besides training. They hadn't wanted to give him the active slot that he had earned, and he refused to enlist as a Private, so he had no choice other than an officer commission in the Inactive Reserves. It was how he was going to enter the competition; he had found a loophole. The competition was open to the *whole* fleet.

The top mech pilot from each major unit could enter. As a member of the Inactive Reserve, he was their top mech pilot. Especially since he was the only one with a mech. As a member of the Inactive Reserves, you were responsible for providing and maintaining your own weapons. His mech, as pieced together and mismatched as it appeared, was a weapon. It was a war machine.

If called to duty, by regulation, the fleet would provide ammunition or battery clips for Reservists' weapons. They would have to provide the grenade launcher, railgun ammo, and missile racks for his mech. It had been two hundred years since Inactive Reservists had been called to duty, but the regulations still stood. He was an Inactive Reservist, and this was one of his weapons.

* * * * *

Chapter Three

On the morning of the competition, Rinto let Harmon, Clip, and Zerith use his heavy hauler to get the mech to the Star Port, where the competition was scheduled to begin. They were going up in a dropship to drop onto the first part of the competition from ten thousand feet.

When they arrived and unloaded the mech, a major in the Marines came over to them.

"What are you doing? What is this?" Major Audell asked, looking at his roster and back up to the ugliest mech he had ever seen.

Harmon saluted and said, "Lieutenant Tomeral of the Inactive Reserves, sir. Reporting for the competition." Harmon had a good haircut, a shave, and was in his combat fatigues, a light grey mottled pattern.

The major took out his slate and brought up the Inactive Reserves, and, sure enough, there was Lieutenant Tomeral. He also went over the competition regulations several times with a deepening frown.

"Wait here," he said.

He walked over to where other mechs and their pilots were waiting to receive their battle load and ammunition. He spoke to an older officer, who looked over toward them. He was probably a marine colonel. It appeared as if they were arguing, the major pointing again and again at his slate. After several minutes, the colonel threw his hands up and walked away, reaching for his personal comm.

The major walked back over, smiling and shaking his head, and said, "Colonel Keithel is not happy. All of the highest-ranking officers in the fleet will be watching the live competition videos and attending the awards ceremony. When they see this mech and you, an Inactive Reservist, they are not going to be happy. But, the regulations read that you can enter because you are the top mech pilot in the IR. As a matter of fact, I think you are the only one. I hope you do well. I saw in your records where you finished in the order of merit at the academy. Off the record, I think it was dead wrong for them to have put you into the Inactive Reserves. With the initiative you showed today, just to enter like this, we could have used a guy like you. Frost! I could use a guy like you."

By the way he spoke, Harmon could tell he was from Joth. There *were* officers in the fleet from the planet Joth. They were commissioned from other graduate schools with officer training courses. There were just none from the celebrated Tretrayon System Academy. The graduates of that school looked out for their own, and it showed, since all the top brass in the fleet were academy alumni.

Rinto laughed after the major walked away. "I can't believe you're in. Boy, you better win. I'm putting big money on you and this monster," he said.

Rinto Gilthon was a grey-haired man with a drooping mustache. He was approaching eighty years old, but he only looked fifty with the expensive, age arresting procedure he had received. He had spent the first ten years of his adult life as a salvager, collecting scrap in space. He used a ship handed down through several generations in his family until there had been an accident with its fusion drive. The resulting explosion had killed his crew and mangled his right arm as well as damaged his ribs and a lung. He would have died if not for the procedure he had received years earlier. His small ship had limped backed into occupied space. But, by the time he received emergency care, the damage was permanent and medical repair nanites couldn't save his arm or lung.

He opted then to just go with a mechanical arm instead of re-growth. He sold what was left of his ship and started the scrapyard. He decided he didn't need to go back into space with his lung the way it was, anyway.

Rinto had other employees of various races working for him, but he tended to favor Clip and Harmon. Maybe it was because he was a lifelong bachelor with no children of his own that caused him to feel that way. The exposure to the reactor on his ship had made him in-capable of having children of his own. That and the fact the boys didn't have any family but each other because they were orphaned when their town was buried. He didn't let other employees take items from the scrapyard without paying for them. They had told him about the weapons cache he had "given" them, and he had just laughed. He should have listened.

Before Harmon climbed into the mech, Clip stopped him. "Hey, when you go into freefall, call me. I put a few surprises into this thing," he said, patting the thigh of the war machine.

There was no telling what Clip had programmed. "Wait, what did you do?" Harmon asked.

"It iss a ssurprisse," Zerith chipped in, his tail waving.

"Great, the most important thing I have ever done is ahead of me, and you guys are experimenting," he said. Then he laughed, "I guess this whole machine is an experiment. What could go wrong?"

He climbed into the mech, fired it up, and moved over to the ready line to get his missile racks, grenade launcher, and ammunition.

His mech—fourteen feet tall—was huge standing next to the others. The other, more modern mechs were between ten and twelve feet tall with smaller bodies.

In mechs—like everything else—the body and its components had been reduced in size over time, becoming smaller and more compact. The smaller of the two types of mechs present, at ten feet, were used by the Marine Recon units. They were designed to scout ahead, and they were faster and more agile than the others used by the Corps.

He got out to speak to the sergeant in charge of the weapons point when he heard a voice behind him. He recognized the speaker and thought, *here we go*. It was Marteen Yatarward, a classmate from the academy.

"What are *you* doing here, and what in the blazes is *that*? You couldn't make it into the fleet, so you built your own mech?" he asked, as those around him laughed. "It looks like a piece of chinto squat. Probably smells like it inside, too. You're just going to embarrass yourself. Why don't you just pack it up and go home, if it will make it that far?"

Yatarward was an ass, and he always had been. He was one of those people who always put others down to bring himself up. He had probably been a bully in secondary school, as well. Harmon didn't know since Yatarward was from an exclusive beach town on Tretra. His family had old credit, centuries old. Not only was he an ass, he was a bigot, too, and the only reason Harmon hadn't beaten the squat out of him at the academy was a deep-seated fear of losing his scholarship.

Before Harmon could answer, another voice chimed in. It was a feminine voice, and it made him smile. "Why don't you shut your face, Yatarward?" Evelyn Stacey asked. "You're the only one around here who sniffs chinto squat enough to know what it smells like. Besides, what are *you* doing here? I heard your unit didn't really have a tie and was able to enter two mechs. Did you whine and moan your way into a slot? Just like you did to get into the fleet? You went crying to your daddy."

Harmon turned and looked at her. He had not seen her since graduation night two years ago. She, like Harmon and Yatarward, had lieutenant's stripes sewn onto her uniform. She also had another patch that Harmon and Yatarward didn't have. She had become a recon platoon leader in the Marines. Yatarward had simply become a platoon leader in the Marines. His family ties couldn't get him into the recon unit, though, Harmon had heard. Not that he hadn't tried.

She smiled at him and said, "Hey, Stranger."

"Hey, Evelyn, it's great to see you," Harmon said, ignoring Yatarward.

It *was* great to see her. They had dated for the last two years of the academy. She was still just as beautiful. She was easy to talk to and easy on the eyes, with freckles on her nose and a beautiful smile. Her hazel eyes stood out against her dark auburn hair. It was cut short to make it easier to manage in a helmet and in a mech.

They had agreed that a long-distance relationship just wasn't going to work out. With her on active status in the fleet, and him moving back to Joth, they would never find time for each other. It sucked, but it was life. You had to move on, though both regretted it the moment they agreed on the decision.

"Ignore him, he's just afraid you'll beat him again. Like you did at almost everything at the academy," she said, and looked back at Yatarward. "You know good and well that Harmon should be on active status, and you should have gone home. You sure didn't finish in the top fifteen percent. I don't care what your final ranking was. You're probably the reason he didn't get in."

Several of the Marines eased away from the three of them. Officers arguing with each other was not an environment any enlisted Marine wanted to be a part of, even if they were corporals or sergeants. They still listened from a distance, though, because they were curious to hear what was being said.

"He didn't get in because he couldn't cut it. I'm in because I was selected. I didn't screw my way in like some people I know," Yatarward said. Harmon figured Yatarward knew it wasn't true, but the jerk resented her for getting into recon, something he didn't have the skills for.

Harmon balled a fist and stepped toward Yatarward. He was no longer at the academy, and getting an active slot was irrelevant. He was going to give Yatarward the beating he deserved. Evelyn quickly stepped between them.

"He's not worth it. He's just trying to get you kicked out of the competition because he's afraid he can't beat you. It's just words, and you and I know it's not true. Forget him," she said.

"You better pray I don't face you in the combatives," Harmon told Yatarward.

"Whatever," Yatarward said, though he was clearly nervous.

When it was Harmon's turn to arm his machine, the sergeant looked up at it and said, "The lift won't put the missile racks up that high. It's designed to go as high as a twelve-foot mech's shoulder."

"No problem," Harmon said over the external speakers.

He dropped his mech down to one knee as smoothly as a man might kneel so the lift could reach his shoulders. Other pilots watched the exchange and noted how well the mech moved. The longer, older leg design seemed to move better than the new models they had. Even Yatarward noticed it, but he stayed silent.

Harmon received the same equipment every competitor received. The two racks of missiles held nine missiles each. He was given one thousand rounds for his railgun. It was fed from a back compartment through the right arm to the railgun itself. His larger mech could have held more, but he received the same load the other machines did. He was given a grenade rifle with a twenty-round magazine to put into the slot on his left leg. Jump fuel was available if he needed to top off, but Zerith had already made sure he was full. He and Clip had also checked his environmental system. It could pull from outside the machine and deliver filtered air to Harmon, or it could become self-contained for as long as the power held out, and the CO_2 scrubber worked. He was ready.

* * * * *

Chapter Four

The briefing for the mission was held in the hanger directly behind the dropship. The ship being used was the HDS 40, the newest heavy dropship in the Tretrayon Defense Fleet. It could carry forty fully-equipped mechs on board. The ship was designed to quickly descend toward a planet surface and release the war machines at any time. It could, if needed, also provide limited air support for troops on the ground with its forty-millimeter quad machine guns.

There were thirty-four mech pilots in the briefing room, including Harmon. He could tell by their uniforms that most of them were Marines, but there were a few Ground Defense Force pilots in the mix. Those pilots had to be the very best the ground defense had. There were several mech units in the ground defense, but this was a marine competition, so the GDF had only sent a handful of their very best.

Harmon recognized one of the pilots, a GDF Active Reservist. They were under a different command than the Marine Inactive Reserves. Jonoah "Twiggy" Bentalt, had been a classmate of his as well, and he had been commissioned into the Active Reserves, opting to drill once a month and three weeks a year. His family owned a huge farming outfit on Tretra, so he never considered full-time duty. Twiggy looked over at him and crossed his eyes. Good old Twiggy.

"You will drop from ten thousand feet at one-minute intervals," said the major giving the briefing. "There is a target ring at the designated landing site. Control your descent, and do not overshoot the mech ahead of you. Once the first mech hits the ground, the following mech will land no sooner than forty-five seconds later and no longer than one minute, fifteen seconds later. Each mech will follow under the same time structure. This will give you enough time to move out of the drop zone toward the simulated contact. Do not hesitate on the landing site. Get down and get moving."

"Once everyone has moved to the firing range, you will be timed and evaluated on how you eliminate the threats. There will be the standard twenty threats, per the Advanced Mech Qualification Range. The only difference between this and the normal range is that the threats can shoot back. Simulated, of course, but if the computer says you are hit, depending on the location, you will lose points. If the computer determines that you were immobilized, you will lose additional points.

"A destroyed mech does us no good in combat. I suggest you use the terrain to your advantage.

"After the mech range portion of the event, you will move out on a ten-kilometer road march. At the finish line, you will locate the extraction point for the dropship and load up. The dropship will bring you back here where you will dismount and run two miles to an obstacle course. It will be followed by individual marksmanship, firing both the standard grenade rifle and a laser pistol. The day will end with a combatives tournament."

As everyone was jotting down mission notes, the major asked, "Are there any questions?"

Hands shot up all over the room. When he called on the first Marine to raise her hand, he realized his mistake.

"Do you think the Furies have a chance at the System Warball Championships, and what do you think of their new defenseman, Branze Gortrip, who was acquired in a trade with the Dust Devils?" she asked. Snickers could be heard from the back of the room.

"Are there any questions pertaining to the task at hand?" he asked.

* * *

The pilots loaded their mechs into the dropship and backed into slots designed to lock their machine into place. The last thing anyone wanted was a loose mech during high-G maneuvers. It was assumed that anytime a dropship full of war machines was needed, it was a hostile environment. The ships had shields, but they could only take so much before lasers burned through or kinetic rounds overloaded the system. Erratic flight was the first line of defense for a dropship.

Harmon's mech would not lock into place because of its size and shape difference. He countered by reaching back and gripping the bracket with both claws, locking his fists into place. The crew chief, a sergeant, walked the line, checking each bracket before takeoff. He raised his eyebrows at Harmon but moved on. The word had spread that Harmon had found a loophole in the competition, and everyone liked an underdog.

The sergeant climbed the ladder that took him to his drop observation station, a raised area above the door to the cockpit of the craft. He stepped back, hooked his harness to the two secure points behind him, and dropped the visor on his helmet. Ten minutes later, the red lights glowing above him flashed; there was approximately two minutes until drop.

Harmon felt his pulse rate climb a little. He could see it on the operator status portion of his lower left screen. Had he been tied into a command net, his chain of command could have seen it, too. As it was, Clip was the only one looking at it on a custom-built slate, slightly larger than a personal comp.

Harmon double-checked the pin for the coordinates he had entered into his mech system. It put a map overlay onto his center screen, and it provided him with a target to aim for on the ground. It would also let him know how he was doing with time. He didn't want to land outside the designated window and lose points on the first event.

The lights went out for a full second, and when they came back on, they were glowing green. Both sides of the ship's walls dropped like a ramp below the wings, and the first mech exited with a leap. Harmon waited his turn. He was designated as the last to exit. In an actual combat jump, both sides of twenty mechs would exit at the same time and spread apart while free-falling. It was something they practiced monthly. Harmon had only dropped four times in the past while in training. He was a little nervous; maybe it was a good thing they weren't dropping all at once.

Thirty-three minutes later, Harmon leaped from the dropship. He splayed the mech's limbs out to control his fall so he didn't start spinning and cause himself to black out. He checked his display. About eight seconds into the drop, he reached terminal velocity.

He was falling at about 250 feet per second, or about one hundred and seventy miles an hour. He was glad the mech's operating system kept up with all of that. The math for this type of thing had never been his strong suit. Its formula included a planet's gravitational pull, atmospheric density, wind drag, mech position while falling, and other factors that were beyond him. His display showed that he would hit the ground in three minutes and fifty seconds if he did nothing else. Of course, he would alter his drop position to aim for the landing zone and fire his rockets to slow himself down and land, so that time would change slightly. He could see the other mechs below him on visual and on radar.

Harmon called Clip. "Hey Clip, do you read me?"

"I got you loud and clear man. I can see you are falling like a rock. What's it like?" Clip asked.

"It's not as fun as you think it would be. It's happening pretty fast. Why did you want me to call you while I was in freefall?" Harmon asked, wanting Clip to get to the point.

"Well, for one, I have this scrambled, and no one can hear us. Also, Zee acquired a few extra pieces for the hardware in the mech's radar, and I may or may not have hacked the program for a multi-launch command off an experimental anti-air tank," Clip answered back, looking around to ensure no one was near his hovercraft.

"You didn't," Harmon said.

"Yep, orient yourself toward the target range, zoom the visual onto the targets themselves, and lock in eighteen of them. The system will program the coordinates in. When the time comes on the range, fire all your missiles at once. I tweaked the targeting program off of something I read about in combat on Earth in the 1990s. It will save time on the range. Oh, and Zee says you're welcome," Clip said.

Harmon looked toward the range; he only had two minutes left. He zoomed in well beyond the visual range of any mech he had been in before and could see the targets behind berms, edging around corners, and up on a roof in the simulated urban environment. It was amazing his mech could see that far. He selected all of his missiles on both racks. Using the aiming reticle on his screen and finger commands, he chose the first eighteen targets. The system gave him the option of pre-selection or engage. He was careful not to engage yet. He could see all twenty targets from his high-altitude angle. The last two were in the windows of buildings, and he only saw their quad barrels.

Shortly after, he angled his body to guide himself to land on the center circle on his display. He could see that the mech before him had gotten pretty close. Watching his display and trusting the operating system when it counted down, he dropped his feet toward the surface and fired his rockets to slow himself down. To his surprise, the thrust was stronger than the mechs he had trained in, and he was able to slow down and practically fly over to land in the dead center of the circle. He stepped off the landing zone like he owned it.

* * *

In the conference center of the Star Port Hotel, the three-dimensional screen covering one whole wall showed Lieutenant Tomeral in his personal mech land perfectly, without even having to bend knees and compensate for the drop at all. The big ugly mech just strolled off. His name and unit were displayed on the bottom of the screen. The High Command and their staff were watching the competition and enjoying a few drinks.

"What the hell was that? Was that the Inactive Reservist you mentioned, Fritz?" Admiral Timerton demanded. He was livid.

"Yes, sir. That's Lieutenant Tomeral. There's nothing we can do about it. Per the regulations, he had the right to enter the competition. When Lieutenant General Wilton told me about it, I had the legal guys look into it. That lieutenant found a loophole."

Wilton chimed in, "Colonel Keithel should have sent his ass packing, anyway." He was pissed off that someone that should not even be in the competition had shown up his Marines.

Major General Alturn, the ground defense commander, said, "Treval, you know that technically, Tomeral is a Marine. He's just on inactive status."

"Screw that noise, he isn't one of us," General Wilton fired back. "He couldn't cut it and got put in the Inactive Reserves straight out of the academy."

"Actually, he got bumped…all the way out. He is from Joth and was on a scholarship for Warball. He didn't know it, but he had a slim shot at commissioning active, anyway. We have never had an academy officer commission active from the planet Joth. When I received a call from Mr. Yatarward about his son, well, that sealed it beyond just the tradition," Colonel Yato said. He was the current commandant of the Tretrayon System Academy. "He actually finished in the top ten percent," he said.

He didn't have to add that the alumni from the academy held a prejudiced attitude about the tradition. It was the reason that no officer from Joth was ever promoted beyond an O4—a major in the Marines or a lieutenant commander in the Fleet. They never received command beyond company level or of a frigate. This system's fleet would be commanded by Tretrayons, and specifically, academy alumni. Period. End of story.

"He's that Tomeral? I made a few credits off him, betting on the games. Still, he's not active, and I don't like him embarrassing my Corps," Wilton said.

"We have the whole damn system watching this thing, and a monstrosity out there is doing better, so far, than our newest mechs? Maybe I should give Mr. Yatarward a call myself; his damn machines can't match a simple drop that a home-made piece of crap can do," Admiral Timerton said.

Yatarward Corporation was the biggest name in military contracts in the entire system. The company developed and built the mech systems in current use. They had held the contract for the last one hundred and fifty years. If the commander for the entire system called him, he *would* answer without his personal assistant giving the caller the usual runaround.

* * *

Harmon waited near the ready line with the other mech pilots who hadn't gone through the range yet, although he had parked his mech a little distance away from the others. Twiggy walked over to chat.

"What's up buddy? How ya been on this hot ball of dust?" he asked, reaching out to shake Harmon's hand.

"Good, man. It's hot, but it's home," Harmon said.

"I hear ya, but I ain't listenin'. It's too hot for my taste; I'll tell ya right now," Twiggy said, wiping his brow. "How in tarnation do y'all grow anything to eat here? The desert is full of them, but you sure can't eat all these cactuses and scrub brush."

Harmon laughed. "We grow it in cool houses."

"Cool houses? What in the world is a cool house?" Twiggy asked. The farmer in him had to know.

"Well, you know how on your planet, hot houses are for growing things off season?" Harmon asked.

"Yeah, we start seedlings in them. Wait, you mean you have clear-steel houses that are cooler inside than outside so y'all can grow crops? Well, I'll be. That's purty smart. I wonder if my pa would be interested in setting up a farm here. Then we could hang out some-time, and I can get away from Zwella Kinwell. I swear that gal won't leave me alone. I ain't ready to get hitched, ya know?" he said.

Harmon laughed. Twiggy had been dodging Zwella for years. She was from the same farming community he was from. His family raised crops while her family raised chinto, a six-legged riding beast native to their planet. It was like the horses of Earth, just longer in body, with small knobs like horns on its head. Their coloring was always unique, a light brown and green-striped pattern. It was a natu-ral camouflage for the tall grass plains that were native to the area the chinto came from.

"How'd you do on the drop?" Twiggy asked.

The scoring from the drop started at one hundred and lost a point for every meter off the center. None of the pilots had received the points deduction for the timing of the drop, which wasn't sur-prising since they were the best mech pilots in the system.

"Ah, you know. I scored a one hundred," Harmon said.

Twiggy whistled. "Then you're the only one to get it. I know you were a good mech operator in training. But dang, dead-on target after falling from ten miles is more than good; it's really good. Bet the brass ain't none too happy right about now," he said, with a laugh.

Harmon climbed into his mech a little later to get ready for his run downrange. The range was a movement-to-contact, live fire range. It was a simulated town, and the goal was to eliminate the threats as you pass through the town. Scoring was based on time completion. It took about ten minutes on average to get through the range.

The targets were tanks, armored personnel carriers, mechs, and crew-served weapons. All were computer-controlled and on tracks. Several times during the morning, they had been replaced due to damage. The missiles they had been issued were exactly like the real ones, except they didn't have explosives in the warhead; there were paint markers in them, instead. Still, the targets had to be replaced periodically because of the damage caused by the impacts of the missiles and railgun rounds.

The threats could fire back, but they fired blanks, or light, in the case of simulated lasers. If the aiming reticle from a target locked in with enough time to hit a mech, the computer took note. It relayed damage reports to the range controllers. Right before each pilot entered the range, the range control cadre placed ten override markers on their mechs. The shock plugs, if activated, would lock up that limb or weapon if it received enough damage. For too many mistakes, it would lock the entire mech down with a temporary electrical surge. This could be painful to a pilot, but it beat the alternative of real combat.

The scoring started at one hundred after eight minutes on the range. Every twenty seconds beyond that time would cause competitors to lose a point. One point was also lost every time a mech was hit. Five points were lost if something had to be locked down. Ten points were given up if there was a total lockdown. This could happen after a mech fired its final shots and eliminated all threats, so it wasn't a total loss of points. Failure to eliminate all threats, however, was a total loss of points.

The actual town itself was not visible to the pilots until it was time to step up to the wall surrounding the town. To start the range, the pilot had to get his mech over the eighteen-foot wall and clear the town. He had the option of climbing over the wall, jumping over with rocket assists, or finding the entrance. Harmon went last, but had no idea how the other pilots had scored.

Right before he let the controller know that he was ready, Clip called him. "Hey man, those little shock plugs they stuck on you won't have any effect on the mech. Me and Zee have it hard wired against a magnetic pulse, so what they use sure isn't going to work. You might just want to avoid getting hit so they don't find out."

"Great," Harmon answered back. "You're going to get me kicked out of the competition before we can win the prize money."

"Nah, fire off all the missiles on your jump over that wall, and then just hunt down the last two. You got this. Oh yeah, Zee says for you to not worry about fuel consumption. You have larger fuel tanks to go with the more efficient thrust nozzles on that thing. A lot more than a normal mech does. The tanks go up above the normal location in those legs. Come to think of it, that might not be so safe in a real hostile environment. Hey Zee, we gotta…" Harmon heard him talking away from his comm before he cut the call.

He stepped across the ready line and fired his thrusters. He angled up over the wall to the left, looking for a spot to land behind something. There were buildings on both sides of the street. They could provide good cover. He took in everything in an instant, added thrust, and commanded all of his missiles to launch at once. They shot almost straight up into the air. He angled back to the right, going higher than he probably should have. He cut the thrusters to land quickly behind a building. He felt that landing like the one he felt back in the warehouse.

He checked all his warning lights and saw no issues. His radar showed his missiles in flight. *No! Something happened to their guidance, they are supposed to head toward a target not up into the air. This is not good,* he thought. He checked his ordnance screen to ensure all eighteen missiles had fired. They had. Radar now showed them angled back toward the ground and gaining speed. He turned up his outside sensors, and he heard the missiles striking targets. *Alright, Clip!*

Harmon armed his railgun and sprinted down the middle of the street, cutting back and forth with no set pattern. He passed several of the targets with fresh paint on them, with flares burning beside them, showing his rockets had hit them. He saw a flash from a window up ahead, and he jumped. He used his thrusters a touch on landing and shot a ten-round burst into the window. The quad gun stopped firing. As far as he could tell, it had not hit him. He fired his jets and flew to the roof of the same building. It was the tallest one in the mock town. From there, he could see the last quad gun attempting to engage him. It couldn't get a lock on him with the top of the window stopping the upward movement of the barrels. He took it out with a ten-round burst. From there, he sprinted to the other end of the town and strolled over the finish line like he attacked towns every day of his life.

* * *

The admiral and his commanders were still watching the competition on the three-dimensional screen as the mech pilots maneuvered their war machines through the live fire range. A mech would come over the wall and maneuver through the town, engaging targets with the missiles or railgun. Sometimes a pilot would fire several missiles at once if they thought that they could destroy more than one target within sight. All were cautious, and only two of them became completely immobilized. The average time to complete the range was about ten minutes. The pilots were good, and it showed.

Lieutenant General Wilton was pleased with the results his Marines were showing. "That's what I'm talking about, right there! The only mechs destroyed were ground defense forces. I believe you owe me a drink, Rupert," he said to Major General Alturn, smiling.

Alturn wasn't going to just take the ribbing, he was going to get a shot in of his own, even if it wasn't one of his soldiers involved. "Tomeral is up next; don't forget about him. Double or nothing he doesn't get immobilized," he said.

"I'm in on this," Admiral Timerton cut in, still ticked off about the drop results. "There is no way his pile of scrap repeats what it did on the drop. Hell, it's a bigger target than the rest of them were. Besides, he doesn't have the same amount of training time as Wilton's Marines. Yato here says he works at a scrap yard, so there's just no way. If he does, that call is being made. I'll tell you right now."

Rear Admiral Flynn Cothco, sitting with the rest of the officers, didn't add to the conversation. He was the third ranking officer in the fleet. He also oversaw the weapons procurement department, and he knew he was probably going to have to be the one to make that call. He just continued to watch.

"What the…" Lieutenant General Wilton said and was on his feet. He, with the rest of the assembled officers, watched Lieutenant Tomeral light off all his missiles at the apex of a rocket-assisted jump, cut back faster than he should have been able to in midair, and land behind a building. The missiles shot up into the air instead of directly at a target. They rose five hundred feet and then came angling in, spreading apart to strike the top of…eighteen separate targets. Eighteen. And each officer there knew every hit would have been a killing blow. All tanks, armored personnel carriers, and mechs are most vulnerable at their weakest point: the thin top armor. It was where entry hatches were located.

"How, in the all-fired hell, did he just do that? A mech doesn't have that type of missile guidance capabilities. And those rockets…who designed those missiles?" he asked, looking around, his eyes landing on Rear Admiral Cothco.

"The missiles just go where the guidance programming tells them to go. It appears that Lieutenant Tomeral has some custom programming in the operation system of that mech to go with the custom build," Cothco said, clearly intrigued.

They watched as Tomeral ran down the street, jumped, destroyed a crew-served gun, and then flew to the top of the tallest building in the town to destroy the last target. All eyes turned toward the admiral.

"He just completed the range in three minutes. Three. Get me a comm," he said, visibly reddening.

* * *

Tomeral dismounted from his mech and turned to see every mech pilot in the competition watching him, even Yatarward. None of them had ever seen a war machine complete a live fire range in that kind of time. Ever. Twiggy threw him a double thumbs-up, and Evelyn smiled at him, so he winked at her and turned to watch the sergeant and his assistant remove the plugs from his mech.

"Craziest thing I ever saw, Sarge. Three minutes. That must be some kind of record. None of the plugs have been tripped. 'Puter says he didn't get hit once," Harmon overheard the private say. He owed Clip and Zerith a cold one for sure.

The next event was a ten-kilometer, cross country road march. They were given the coordinates for the dropship pick up, which they locked into their map overlay. It showed where the pickup point was. It was over some rough terrain, ending at what appeared to be a small mountain.

The mechs bunched up at the starting line like a group of marathon runners. It wasn't a marathon, but it wouldn't be easy. To go that kind of distance in a mech quickly took considerable effort. Not near as much as running it themselves, though. The starting flare flew into the air, and the mechs were off.

Harmon had started at the back of the group. He didn't want his machine jostled. As the pack spread out, he could see that Evelyn and other scout mechs like hers were pulling ahead as they maneuvered around boulders and into and out of ravines and gullies. The smaller mechs were designed to be fast, but his machine's longer strides started making up ground as he went.

He watched a few of the pilots up ahead opt to use the remainder of their rocket fuel to assist them in jumping across some of the deeper ravines. This worked out well for them until they burned up the last of their fuel. Most of them had already used all of it on the drop and in the town. He looked at his gauge. He still had a quarter of his fuel left. He decided to hold it in reserve, just in case.

He continued to gain ground on the mechs ahead of him and began passing them with his longer stride. In the ravines, he took advantage of the extra two feet in height. He used his claws while digging in the mech feet and was able to quickly scramble out of them. This let him catch and pass even more of the mechs. All that time in the grappler was paying off in his climbing technique.

As he got closer to the finish line, he could see that it was not at the base of the mountain. It was, actually, one hundred and fifty feet up on a cliff side. The cliff was large enough to have the dropship sitting on top, waiting. *Nice, a little wrinkle at the end of this event.*

There were only four mechs ahead of him as he was approaching the vertical wall two hundred yards away, and one had already begun climbing. He thought it was Evelyn, but he wasn't sure. He called Clip.

"Hey Clip, you there?" he asked over the comms, between breaths.

"No, he iss not. He went to get a beer. I have his sslate and commss," Harmon heard Zerith say.

"I've got a quarter tank…left for the rockets…is that enough to go…say one hundred and fifty feet…straight up?" Harmon asked, breathing deep between phrases, figuring if anyone knew, Zerith would.

"Yess, I designed the thrusterss myself. They are fuel-efficient and powerful. When I make ssomething, it iss made right," Harmon heard him say, as if his feelings were hurt.

"Well, alright then…my friend…I'm about to take this event…too," he said, breathing even harder.

Harmon jumped from about fifty feet in front of the cliff wall, fired his thrusters at their maximum output, and flew past the climbers. He went up the cliff wall, eased over, and landed as if it was just another step, to the astonishment of the graders and the pilots standing outside the ship. The crew chief gave him the double pump signal with a balled fist from within the open ramp of the dropship. He had stayed in the shade under a vent to stay cool. Harmon was panting and sweating heavily despite the cool air circulating through the war machine. He strode over and into the dropship like the jump was nothing special.

* * *

There was silence at the table in the conference center. All assembled had just watched the ugly mech with Lieutenant Tomeral piloting it, run down every mech in the race, fly past the ones he didn't catch, and land softly on the cliff. Tomeral strode into the dropship out of sight.

Wilton threw his beer across the room, and his aide moved to clean it up. "Son of a…how the hell did he just do that? You mean to tell me that he had enough rocket fuel to fly that big ass mech up one hundred and fifty feet with fuel to spare for a perfect landing? After the maneuvering he did in the town? Chinto squat! I call chinto squat! I want to know if somebody snuck him some fuel, and I want to know now!" he said, looking around for another aide to task.

Admiral Timerton was so mad that he was calm. "He did. And no, he did not refuel. The cameras have been on all the men and women in this competition at all times. It appears as if he, and *whoever* he has helping him, have built a better mech. And...he is one hell of a pilot. Why does he have to be from Joth?" he asked.

"Who *has* been helping him with the design?" Colonel Yato wondered out loud. He turned to his aide, a lowly major in a room full of command officers. "Find out if there have been communications from that machine and to whom." The major stepped over to a corner of the room and engaged her slate.

She came back over to the table, as they watched the last of the mechs boarding the dropship. "Sir," she said, "he has communicated. We can see where transmissions were made. But they are scrambled, and intel can't unscramble them. It is an algorithm unlike anything they have seen before. When they think they are getting close, it is as if the algorithm knows and changes. They have been working on it since the drop, when they first detected the scrambled signal."

At this, Commander Melanie Fritz raised her eyebrow. She had been silent during most of the day, as was her usual disposition. Intelligence officers seldom volunteered anything or spoke out of place. She would be looking into this. *Unbreakable indeed*, she thought, reaching for her comm.

* * *

Harmon parked the mech close to where they had unloaded it from Rinto's heavy hauler. Clip and Zerith were there to check the machine and see how it had stood up to everything. The empty missile racks, the remainder of the rounds for the railgun, and the rifle had been turned in to the ammo point already. As he walked away, he saw Zerith's feet and tail sticking up out of the open hatch. *I hope he doesn't drip any of that spazzel fruit in there,* he thought, shaking his head. *Even though he's a vegetarian, Zerith is always eating something. You'd think they'd eat light.*

All the pilots were preparing to make the two-mile run to the obstacle course—ensuring their boots were clasped tight and drinking water or energy drinks. As soon as they crossed the finish line, they would start the course. The run and the obstacle course combined for a score based on time. Harmon drank some water. He didn't want to feel the energy ebb once the drinks wore off.

Unlike the road march, the pilots didn't gather up at the starting line. Like the drop, they were at one-minute intervals. Harmon was slated to go last again. There was no sense in burning out in a sprint at the beginning of the run; he planned to run his standard six-and-a-half-minute per mile pace and hoped to make up some time on the obstacle course. He had always done well on it at the academy.

He knew this was the one event he wouldn't win. His average total score for the entire day would have to make up for it. He knew for a fact there were some serious runners in the group. Would they set records? No, but then again, they were running in boots and fatigues. Evelyn was one of the best runners, and he had seen her run a six-minute pace for two miles several times. She always beat him.

He listened to the timekeeper count down, and then he was off. The course was well-marked all the way to the obstacle course. He didn't catch the runners he could see ahead of him, but he didn't fall back either. He looked ahead and saw the course started with a wall. *Great,* he thought. The wall was followed by many more obstacles.

* * *

Harmon swung across the pit on the rope, and sprinted across the finish line. He had passed four other competitors on the course and had almost caught another. He was drinking more water and thinking about the rifle range when the results were posted. His finishing time was tenth. He was glad to get it. It was not a bad score for not having an obstacle course to train on. He wondered if this course would be left in place after the competition; he wouldn't mind working out on it every now and then.

On the rifle range, all thirty-four competitors were able to compete at once. They used grenade rifles, the standard issue for a mech pilot. The grenade rifles would allow any pilot that had to eject from a mech the ability to still cause major damage, like their mech would have. The competitors only used twenty dummy rounds on the range and not the full load that would be available to a mech pilot in combat, though.

Harmon watched as the last of his grenades sailed through the twelve-inch slot, one hundred meters away. *Not bad*, he thought. Every grenade had gone right where he had aimed. *Not bad at all.* He checked and cleared his grenade rifle, slung it on his back, and strolled off the range. The range for the laser pistol was just a formality, really. Every mech pilot there was deadly accurate with a pistol. The range had thirty targets at various ranges. They had to change battery packs after the fifteenth round, and that's where the separation in shooters' abilities began—how fast the competitors reloaded was crucial.

There were four different types of pistols Harmon saw being used. The type of pistol a Marine used depended on what the unit issued for some of them, and for others, on personal preference. The recon units were pretty lenient with their Marine's choices, if they got the job done. Harmon's pistol was completely different from all the others. His was, what he liked to call, his Zerith special.

Zerith had taken apart one of the pistols from the weapons cache they found to see how it was put together. He quickly realized he could take the grip of one of Harmon's other pistols and fit it to the new weapon. The battery clip on the alien pistol slid into place under the barrel like the pump on an antique hunting shotgun, a weapon Clip had shown to him one evening when they were having a few beers. A normal laser pistol had a battery pack that you clipped into place in front of the trigger. Changing the alien pistol's charge pack was a smooth motion: depress the release with a finger from the hand gripping it, hold the new pack with two fingers on the free hand, slide the used pack off and let it drop, and slide the charged one on. Just like pumping a shotgun.

Harmon had practiced the move over and over in their apartment. Compared to a regular pistol, there was no doubt it was faster. When he performed the move during his turn on the range, it looked like he had been doing it for years. He had the best time by more than a second. Noticing the range sergeant's look, he nodded, holstered his pistol, and stepped off the range like he owned it.

* * *

Major General Alturn was laughing. "Did you see that? I have never seen someone reload the pack on a pistol that fast. What kind of pistol was that, anyway? Wilton, do you know?" he chided, knowing Wilton was ready to explode, again.

"Who the hell knows!" Lieutenant General Wilton exclaimed, throwing his arms up. "Tomeral has all kinds of squat that my Marines are not issued. It should be a disqualifier," he said.

Admiral Timerton said to the group in a serious voice, "No. It is not a disqualifier because he is an Inactive Reserve officer. The IR provide their own weapons. There is nothing in the regulations that says he can't use that particular pistol. He has just outshot the best we have, right before our eyes. People, he is going to win this competition. Hell, he came in tenth on the run and obstacle course, and he is still so far ahead, it's laughable." He turned to Colonel Yato with anger in his eyes. "Yato, tell me. Can he fight? Is he going to embarrass us all, once again, in combatives?"

Yato was silent for a moment, not wanting to be the bearer of bad news. He finally spoke without looking at them. "Harmon Tomeral grew up in an orphanage center. It's all there in his bio. He has had to fight his entire life. You all know what life is like in places like that. We have all seen the videos depicting them. Or, unfortunately, when they hit the system news for something awful. Older kids trying to take what little you have—food, toys…whatever," he said, and looked up at them. "Tomeral never lost a combatives match while at the academy. Ever. He beat *all* the academy combative instructors, starting from the first lesson. That's the day when the instructors do a little wall-to-wall counseling to let the cadets know "what's what." His junior year, he was a peer instructor. His senior year, the primary instructor. Yes, sir…he will embarrass us."

* * *

There were thirty-four competitors. That meant the first round would have seventeen fights. Two of the competitors, by random drawing, would have to fight two fights in the first round. The second round would be eight fights, then four, then two, and then the final pairing. Each fight was five minutes long. The fight would be won by points, knockout, or submission. There were few rules: no strikes to the groin area, no strikes to the neck, no eye gouging. There were no weight classes. All fights were by random draw. This part of the competition awarded points per win.

The combatives, the last part of the competition, was the most watched part of the competition. It was broadcast on both planets in the system, as well as available on the net, so the members of the fleet stationed off-planet could watch. Many wagers had been made.

The entire system had been abuzz with the story of the IR Marine dominating the competition. On Tretra, the commentators for the event discussed whether Lieutenant Harmon Tomeral should have been allowed to compete. News anchors were doing the same thing. They brought retired members of the fleet, some that had even contended in the competition in years past, in for their opinion. For the most part, the spin was not positive for Tomeral. Some stations didn't even attempt to hide their contempt for someone from the "lesser" planet in the system.

There were quickly-put-together hit pieces on the fact he provided his own weapons. On Tretra, citizens could not own pistols at all. Long gun licenses were extremely limited to the rural areas of the planet where the dangers of native animals were a real concern. They only briefly went over the fact that even on their planet, the IR members were required by fleet regulations to own their own weapons.

On the planet Joth, the news was the exact opposite. The stories highlighted the fact that one of their own was far in the lead. Of course, a native of Joth was going to win the shooting parts of the competition. Weapons, weapon safety, and target shooting were taught in all the schools. The speculation was that Harmon Tomeral was going to win the combatives portion of the competition, too. Families across the planet were prepared to let their children stay up late until the awards ceremony was complete.

By now, Harmon had no illusions on how the first round was going to go. He *knew* that he would be one of the ones selected to have to fight two fights in the first round. He also knew that he would be in the last match, followed immediately with the extra match if he won. He didn't care.

Fighting had always come naturally to Harmon. He had been raised with three older brothers that would wrestle and box each other, including their youngest brother. His family didn't believe in "letting the little one win." If you won or lost, it was on your own merit. The fact that someone was older or bigger was irrelevant. You either became good enough to win or you lost. Living on the edge of the wastelands, there was no room for leniency. Life was tough, so toughen up.

He carried that with him into the orphanage after he lost his family in the storm. It was a good thing he did, too. He was able to protect himself and his best friend, Clip. It didn't take long for the word to spread. They were a pair that you didn't steal from, bully, or...any of the other things that happened in those places. Though, every now and then, a new someone, or a group of new someones, would move into the orphanage center and try. Often, they were moved into the center because they were uncontrollable wherever they came from. They would arrive, thinking they could run the center like they did their last one, only to painfully find out their plans would have to change.

As the matches were proceeding, Harmon saw Twiggy lost his fight on points. Twiggy, at six feet four, had the reach on his shorter opponent and wouldn't allow himself to be taken to the mat. He kept his stance wide and balanced his upper body accordingly. It didn't make for an appealing fight, and the points awarded showed it.

Evelyn won her match in the first minute when she caught the much larger man she was fighting with a kick to the side of the head. He folded like a sack, having become overconfident because of their size difference. He didn't realize the speed of her kick was more than enough to compensate for it. Harmon was glad she kept some of the things he had taught her in mind: show no fear, use your opponent's eagerness against them, and sometimes the best defense is an aggressive offense.

Harmon's first match was the last of the first round. He stepped into the ring and looked over at his opponent. The man he was facing was huge. At easily six feet eight and made of solid muscle, this match was not going to be something he took lightly. *The fix is in,* thought Harmon. The man on the other side of the ring was the biggest person in the competition. *The way he is bobbing and weaving over there and warming up, the guy knows what he is doing.* Harmon watched him closely and smiled to himself. He realized the man's weakness.

They touched gloves at the center of the ring, when the referee said, "fight." Harmon noticed that there was no malice in his opponent's eyes. If the fix was in, the man had nothing to do with it. He was just fighting whoever was selected by the officials. They nodded in respect and began circling and feeling each other out.

Harmon did the last thing that the big man, as well as everyone watching the fight, had expected. He shot in low, wrapped his arms around the man's buttocks and upper thighs, pulled hard toward himself, and lifted with all his leg strength. By pulling against himself and lifting, his own legs became the only contact with the mat for both men. His opponent reacted by instinct and attempted to push away from Harmon's bear hug. This aided Harmon's surprise move, and the big man went down hard.

The man was dazed because the back of his head struck the mat with Harmon's added weight on him, and his defense was nonexistent. Harmon half-stood and came down with a blow to his face that ended the fight. Harmon stepped over to the side, while the referee checked the man and officially stopped the match. There had been no reason for Harmon to continue to rain blows on the helpless Marine; he knew when he struck that the fight was over. It had lasted fifteen seconds.

When Harmon stepped into the ring for the extra fight of the first round, the man across the ring had an inquisitive look on his face. He was well-rested since he had fought and won the first fight of the evening. He was about the same size as Harmon at six-two and two hundred and thirty pounds, but he was decidedly older. With his experience in the Marines and having watched Harmon fight, he knew he was going against someone that didn't fit any type of fighting mold. Harmon could read the man's face and guess what his thoughts were and then see when the man second-guessed what he had just thought. Harmon knew what he was going to do.

When the ref said "fight," Harmon touched gloves with him and went straight into boxing mode. He threw several left-hand jabs at the man's face, causing his opponent to block the punches. Harmon threw a right to his head; it was blocked, also. Harmon threw three more jabs in a row, and when he felt the man was expecting the right, he caught his opponent with a powerful shot into the man's lower ribs with his left hand. Harmon heard the air whoosh out of him, and as the man bent to that side in obvious pain, he stepped a little to the right, twisted, and caught the side of the man's head with a crushing downward punch. The older Marine was unconscious before he hit the mat.

* * *

Inside the conference center, it was quiet. They had watched Lieutenant Harmon Tomeral knock out two of their best fighting Marines. In total, the fights had lasted twenty-five seconds. Tomeral was embarrassing them.

No one said a word as they looked over to Admiral Timerton. Even Major General Alturn decided that now was not the time to tease Lieutenant General Wilton. Tomeral was going to win the entire competition. It was no longer in doubt.

"Commander Fritz, I want to know about the programming in that mech. I want to know who helped him build it. I want to know how they can scramble their communications to an extent that we can't unscramble them. I want to know about that pistol. I want it yesterday," Admiral Timerton said. He was going to have to explain to the system president why someone from Joth—someone that wasn't even on active status—had embarrassed the entire fleet and the citizens of Tretra. The look in his eyes let everyone at the table know how he felt.

"I'm already on it, sir," she answered back.

"Wilton, we have no choice but to have the ceremony and present Tomeral with the trophy. I want it to be a quick ceremony. It pisses me off to do it, *and* we must give the man 100,000 credits, too. What can we do about that?" Timerton asked the group.

"Well, sir…" Rear Admiral Cothco said.

* * *

The second round of fights finished with Evelyn losing on points. Her opponent had been an even match for her, and the women were exhausted afterwards. Both were from recon, different units, and they hugged it out after the fight with no hard feelings.

Harmon won his fight by submission. The man he fought had shot toward him but was unable to get him to the mat. Harmon allowed their momentum to carry them to the wall of the cage, and then he slipped under and to the side of the man, dropping down with the man's arm wedged. He used his legs for extra leverage, and the defense force soldier tapped out.

Harmon faced the woman that had beaten Evelyn in the next round. He didn't want to strike her in the face, but he would have, as that was the nature of military combatives. Gender was irrelevant. She threw a kick to his thigh, and he stepped back, slapping her foot hard to cause her to keep turning off balance. He quickly slipped behind her and put her in a sleeper hold. She realized her predicament and tapped before she went under. As they exited the ring, she smiled and nodded. It was both an acknowledgement of his fighting ability and a thank you. She knew what he could have done to her in the ring but chose not to.

Harmon was in the semi-finals. He noticed that Yatarward had lost in the last round. He wouldn't get to face him in the combatives. It was too bad. He wondered if Yatarward had lost his match on purpose so that he wouldn't have to step into the ring with him. His opponent was a shorter man, wide at the shoulders with a low center of gravity.

Harmon decided to fight this one standing up. He kept the man from getting inside his reach with a flurry of punch combinations. The Marine was clearly frustrated, as he preferred to fight in close or on the ground. His frustration got the best of him, taking his mind out of the fight, and Harmon sent him reeling with a kick to his head. Harmon rushed in and finished him with a technical knockout when the referee decided the man was no longer safely defending himself from Harmon's punch combinations.

The final fight of the night started with five minutes more rest than the other fights had. Harmon's competition was shorter than him, at an even six feet. Harmon had watched several of his fights, and he knew the man was fast. Very fast. For this one, he decided to use brute strength.

As soon as the match started, Harmon came in close, eliminating the man's fast hands. When he got inside the man's reach, he enveloped him in the type of clinch that tired fighters use. He then lifted and fell back, slinging the man and turning. He landed on top of him and was able to straddle the man and rain elbows on his head, as the man attempted to control Harmon's hands. It didn't take long for

Harmon to land the first disorienting blow, and the referee stopped it shortly thereafter.

* * * * *

Chapter Five

After the fights, everyone showered and changed back into their fatigues. All of the competitors came by Harmon's assigned locker and congratulated him before they headed into the bar at the convention center. Everyone but Yatarward, that is.

Harmon, Twiggy, Evelyn, and her friend Sergeant Joslyn Whaley were having a beer while they waited for the awards ceremony. Evelyn had introduced Joslyn to them a few minutes earlier. Sergeant Whaley had insisted they call her JoJo if they didn't mind fraternizing with a lowly non-commissioned officer.

"I don't mind at all," Twiggy said, smiling at her.

"Well, since you did almost fall asleep in my arms, I think we can do away with the regulations," Harmon said, raising his beer and causing the pale redhead's cheeks to blush.

"Let's not get too friendly, now," Evelyn admonished, smiling to herself. "I still lay claim."

"Don't worry about it," JoJo said, looking over at Twiggy. "I like them tall and lean."

"Well, alrighty then," Twiggy said, grabbing his beer. He put his arm around her and walked her to the nearest table. "How 'bout we get to knowing each other a bit."

Harmon and Evelyn caught up on old times for the half hour they had to wait until the awards ceremony. She told him about life in the fleet, making recon, and being a platoon leader. He told her of coming back to Joth, how Clip was doing, and about moving in with Zerith. She laughed when he told her that he had no idea where Zerith stuffed all the fruit and vegetables he ate. She said she wanted to meet him.

It didn't take long for them both to feel the same closeness they shared at the academy. He told her of his plans to purchase a ship with his friends and become salvagers. He admitted it was a way to make a lot of credits, but she knew it wasn't a desire of his to get rich; it was his desire to get into space. It was something the fleet had denied him, even though he had earned the right. In a way, she envied him; he would leave the system through the gate. That was something she hadn't been able to do.

The Tretrayon Defense Fleet was just that, a defense fleet. She had, however, heard rumors that some of the fleet might go fight for another system. It would be a historical event if it happened as the fleet had not left the system for two hundred years. She told him of the rumors.

* * *

Specialist Grant Lowantha was in civilian clothes. It was just one of the many uniforms he wore as a counter intelligence specialist in the fleet. Sometimes he even wore other systems' military uniforms, depending on his assignment. He rarely did any work within the home system. He specialized in retrieving electronics, programming, and the occasional piece of equipment. He then had them smuggled back to Tretra for reverse engineering. He just so happened to be in the system and attending the festivities around the competition when he received the coded message. He was working tonight.

Having never been one to question orders, he eased over to the strange mech parked by a civilian transport. After observing the machine and the area with both his own senses and a sweep with a sophisticated slate, he determined that no one was anywhere near the area. They were all inside watching the combatives and getting ready for the awards ceremony. He heard the crowd roar after one of the fights and figured he had at least an hour before anyone came back. All the other mechs had been loaded onto the dropship to be taken back to Tretra after the ceremony. The ship had been locked up, so there was no reason for security to be at the hanger.

He eased over to the mech, climbed up the leg, and opened the cockpit so he could hack into the operating system. His orders were to download everything, including the software for the missile deployment and the comms. The hatch did not appear to be locked. He opened it and received the shock of his life, as a Prithmar pushed a small laser pistol barrel between his eyes.

"Hello, iss there ssomething I can help you with?" Zerith asked.

"I…I," stammered the military spy.

"You will now climb down sslowly and keep your handss where I can ssee them," Zerith said.

The embarrassed spy, one who had countless successful missions under his belt, stood with his hands up as a Prithmar called someone on his comm. The barrel never wavered. Lowantha noticed it was a smaller version of the weapon he had seen on the video, the same type that the IR entrant had used. He had no doubt it was accurate and deadly. *Commander Fritz is not going to be happy*, he thought.

Rinto and Clip arrived shortly after the calls were made. Rinto was livid. Clip just smiled; he knew what the man had been up to. Someone wanted to know what made the mech tick. He would find out who. He eased over behind the man while his attention remained on the pistol, still steadily aimed at him, even though its holder was eating a large yellow vegetable and crunching happily. Clip's fingers flew across his slate, and he proceeded to copy everything from the man's slate from a few feet away.

When Star Port Security arrived, Rinto explained to them what had occurred, and they hauled the man off to jail. Clip provided them with a film clip taken from the mech before they left. This was the planet Joth, and any type of thievery was dealt with accordingly.

They told the man as they put him into the back of their hovercraft that he was lucky he wasn't armed when he attempted to enter the mech. On Joth, that could have gotten him shot with few questions asked, which was one of the reasons the crime rate was so much lower on Joth than Tretra. As the officer explained this, he stretched his consonants. His human partner agreed.

"What do you think that was all about?" Rinto asked them.

"I do not know," Zerith said. "I wass watching Harmon win hiss lasst fight on my sslate and eating a piece of Joobla. I had the mech in passsive mode. Perhapss I sshould have waited to call the authoritiess. We could have found out." There was a sparkle in his eyes.

"I got everything off his slate, so we'll know when we get back home, that's for sure," Clip said. He was looking at his slate. "Well, now, isn't that interesting. It's encrypted," he said, looking up at his friends.

* * *

The ceremony went quickly. The top five entrants were awarded. Admiral Timerton himself handed Lieutenant Tomeral the trophy and posed with him for a photo, though he never said a word. An aide explained that the credits would be deposited and available the next day, then he quickly scurried off. Harmon stuck around and answered some questions from the local news teams on Joth. None of the teams from Tretra interviewed him.

He, Twiggy, and their two dates for the evening walked over to the hauler as Zerith was walking it onto the bed. He jumped on every chance he got to operate it, which was why he had been in it, watching the matches. He had to look up at the screens while he was inside, since the harness and padding had been custom made for Harmon, but he did all right.

Harmon introduced everyone. Zerith jumped down off the hauler and shook hands with the ladies and Twiggy. Clip had met everyone but JoJo in the past. Rinto smiled and stuck out his mechanical hand to shake. He seldom thought of it as anything but a part of him.

His friends told Harmon of the attempted break in. Twiggy said it may have been someone from Yatarward Corporation trying to gain information on the mech. The women didn't say anything; they both suspected the fleet was involved. Being on active duty, they had heard that some of the technology for their new equipment had been gained from outside the system. Some of the advancements and modifications had come too fast for them to have been developed organically.

They all went to the warehouse and pulled the hauler into the bay, although they didn't bother to unload it. The group celebrated the win, telling stories about each other and their past. Clip turned up his music box and introduced the visitors to twenty-first century music, and Twiggy attempted to drink one of the Prithmar beers. He stopped after three sips.

"That's like taking shots, Zee," Twiggy said, shaking his head and sticking his tongue out to cool it. He had taken to calling Zerith as Zee, like Clip did. Everyone laughed at him.

* * * * *

Chapter Six

The next morning, they were all woken up by pounding on the door of the bay. When Harmon opened the small door to see what was going on, he was surprised to see a military hauler, its driver, a commander, and several fleet masters at arms outside.

"What is going on, ma'am?" he asked the commander.

"I am Commander Fritz, and I have come to take your mech to the technical lab on Tretra to determine how it defeated the most modern mechs in the fleet, Lieutenant," she said as if there was no choice in the matter. "According to regulations, FR-1650, Subset A, Section 1, any weapon belonging to an Inactive Reserve member may be brought in and serviced at the fleet's convenience," she quoted. "I will also require the pistol used in the competition."

Before he could answer her, the bay door started to open. Harmon looked over and saw Rinto was the one who had opened it. Rinto had been right behind Harmon as he opened the smaller door and had heard what the woman had said.

"Miss," Rinto said. "I don't care what regulation you quote from. I am not in the fleet. This is Joth, and you can't just take something that belongs to someone else, even if you do work for the system government. It doesn't work that way here."

"That mech…" she started to say.

"That mech belongs to me. I bought it last night from Harmon. I paid good credit for it and the pistol. They both belong to me. Now, if you'll have your people move that hauler, I'll be on my way," he interrupted with a smile.

She stared at him and didn't move, resolve in her eyes. It was clear she was trying to figure a way around this complication.

"Are you going to move, or do I need to call the mayor?" he asked. "Me and Kizoola go way back. I play a monthly game of cards with him and his parent. Been friends for years," he explained.

She turned and motioned to her men, they loaded up, and drove away. The last thing she wanted was for the local law enforcement to get involved. It was bad enough she had to get Specialist Lowantha out of jail last night. She didn't want the mayor of the capital city on the planet to get involved, too. There was no telling who the Prithmar knew at the planetary level of government, either. It was bad enough that the government of Joth was constantly inquiring about the fact that no races, other than humans, were in the Tretrayon Defense Fleet. The planet had offered to provide a full diverse crew from within its citizenship, but that would never happen. It was a touchy subject within the system, and she would not be the one to fuel that fire.

"What was that all about?" Clip asked, rubbing his eyes.

"Well, we know who was all-fired up about getting into the mech last night, now don't we," Twiggy said.

"Well, as far as they're concerned, it's mine, and they can't have it," Rinto said with a wink. "Say, could I keep it here in your warehouse, Zerith?" he asked.

"Abssolutely, I inssisst. My parent will have to charge you the ssame amount that you paid for it, though," Zerith answered, the corners of his mouth turning up in a close imitation of a human smile.

The women laughed at them, though Evelyn was curious as to what fleet would try next. She, Twiggy, and JoJo got ready to leave as the dropship was scheduled to depart at 1200. She went out to say goodbye to Harmon, who was standing by the mech.

"We don't need to wait so long to see each other, you know," he said to her.

"I know, but we both thought it was best. We were wrong. I plan on coming to see you every chance I get, now. If you are not off-planet salvaging, that is. You better let me know when you will be around," she said, lightly punching his chest.

"I will," he said, with a smile. "Hey, that reminds me; I need to check my credit account."

Harmon brought up his account on his slate. There was no new deposit showing in it. There definitely was not one for 100,000 credits, and he could tell something wasn't right. He used his comm to call the number he was given for the finance office last night after the ceremony.

They stood by as he connected with the finance office, and he proceeded to get the run around for ten minutes. When he finally reached someone that could answer his questions, he became furious.

After the call, he threw his comm onto the couch. Everyone had heard one side of the conversation, but they waited to hear the whole story.

"Those bastards!" he exclaimed. "They paid me the prize money all right, but they deposited it into my military pay account. It was deposited at 2500 per regulations, the private just told me. That was the one I cussed at like a squiffle. Poor kid. I mean, it wasn't his fault the brass decided to screw me over. I knew it was too good to be true."

"Your military account? But that can't be accessed without adding an active duty code number for any request," JoJo said, puzzled.

"One Harmon does not have and will not have unless the IR gets activated and he is called to duty," Evelyn explained to the civilians in the room.

"The last time it was an active account, I was at the academy and received a monthly stipend," Harmon said. "Those bastards," he added again.

"All the work and all of our plans just went right out the chute," Clip lamented, sitting down. "I should hack their entire pay system and fry it," he added, talking to himself.

Twiggy looked at Harmon. He knew from the limited times that he had spent with Clip that if anyone could do that, he could. JoJo looked back and forth at them, unsure of what to say.

* * * * *

Chapter Seven

Later that afternoon, after Evelyn, JoJo, and Twiggy had left with promises to stay in touch, the four natives of Joth sat down in the bay. Clip was working on the alien cube they had discovered a few weeks back. It was the first time he'd had a chance to examine it; the preparations for the competition had taken up all his previous time.

Rinto looked at the two young men he thought of as his own. "Let me tell you what we're about to do. I'm going to talk to Yarkle. It's a strange being, having no gender and all, but it's a reasonable being. It told me last time it dropped off a load that it was nearing the end of its life cycle and had no offspring to leave its ship to. It wanted to know if I wanted to buy its ship. It was kind of pricey since it is a decent-sized hauler. I told it no thanks; I was through salvaging a long time ago. I would have mentioned it to you three a while back, but it was more than you could afford, even with the prize money."

"Frost," Rinto added, running his good hand through his hair. "I'm not getting any younger myself. If you boys sell me your scrap and pay me…oh, say, five percent of profit off anything else you find, I'll buy his ship and sell it to you for a credit. It's already registered in the system and with the galaxy, so you can use it to go through the gates. Transferring a title is easy if something is already registered."

Harmon didn't know what to say. Clip had stopped what he was doing and looked over to Rinto. Zerith stopped chewing his snack. The bay was silent.

"This is…we…I," Harmon stuttered.

"Aww, don't make it all mushy, boy," Rinto said. He could see the emotions in Harmon's eyes, feelings that Harmon had no control over, and Rinto didn't want to embarrass him.

"Screw that," Clip said, as he came over and hugged Rinto. Rinto held onto him and patted his back.

"I cannot wait to tell my parent," Zerith said. "I am going to sspacce. Very few in our family go to sspacce. Only the oness transsporting the atmossphere equipment go, and that iss only to enssure complete sshipment and to provide guidancce on the equipment upon arrival." He was practically bouncing, his tail flicking back and forth.

"Well, Clip," Harmon said, "we're going to need you to get on the net and see what you can find out about Yarkle's ship. I know it's an old ore hauler made in the Yvent system. Yarkle converted it to haul scrap instead of ore. It seemed to handle pretty well when I watched it land the last time it brought down a load. I have no idea what it is capable of out of the atmosphere. Speaking of which, make sure you check the schematics on its environmental systems. Yarkle breathes air like we do, but it may be tweaked to more of what its home world ratio has. It's already going to smell like a squat beetle, I can tell you." Yarkle was a Wend, a race that resembled a six-foot-tall beetle standing upright on its back two legs.

Clip stopped what he was doing and sat down with his slate, his fingers flying across it. He was curious to know what type of computer system the ship had, what he needed to modify, or if he needed to reprogram the entire system. "I'm on it," he said, already lost in reading.

"You're going to have to change out the seats in the ship," Rinto added. "I wouldn't doubt that Yarkle had them swapped out or modified to fit itself. It has a crew of four Leethog on the ship, so you may want to think about modifying the crew's quarters too. You know they sleep in those hammock things up in the corner of their rooms." A Leethog was a race of marsupial-analogue beings, who preferred the lighting to be dim but were generally great workers.

"We may want to conssider keeping them ass crew," Zerith said. "I can modify or change the sseatss on the operationss deck with no problem. I will locate ssome thingss," he added, pulling out his slate.

There was a lot of planning to do before the Wend came back into their system. Rinto put a private message on the net so it would reach Yarkle if it was within a gated system. It wasn't cheap, but it was necessary so the guys could get the ship and leave the system before the fleet tried some other plan to get Harmon's mech.

Over the next two weeks, Zerith located several pieces of equipment for the operations center and quarters of the ship. From what he and Clip could tell, the ship's design was one that could be reconfigured for many different races to fly. The Yvent was a race that seldom ventured out of its own system but did a booming business in small to medium-size shipbuilding. Many working-class ships came from there, as the Yvent built them to last.

Two of the seats came from Rinto's warehouse. He maintained a warehouse at the scrapyard where he sold used parts. Sometimes it was panels, other times, it was a door or a seal. His inventory changed all the time, and there was never an inventory sheet. Beings just came in and browsed. It wasn't really a money maker, but Rinto just couldn't see melting down salvageable parts. It also gave him something to do while his employees worked out in the heat of the yard and in the melting factory.

He was surprised when Zerith walked in, went straight to the back, and moved something to take a look at some seats. He didn't bother to ask how Zerith knew right where to find them; Zerith had ways of acquiring things through his network of family and friends that boggled his mind. Rinto wouldn't let him pay for the seats.

Harmon spent some time looking at the ship's layout. The schematics of that model had been easy for Clip to download, although Harmon didn't ask whether it was something readily available to everyone, or if Clip had hacked into the shipbuilding company's internal network. He needed to talk to Clip and Zerith first, but he thought he figured out how to put in an arms room and a ready room for the mech in the main bay of the ship. It would come in handy on salvage jobs where there was no atmosphere. He decided to ask if they could rig a laser on the left arm to cut pieces of salvaged ships down to manageable sizes.

Clip studied the type of computer and programming that normally came in that type of ship. The basic programming was fine for what they intended, but he saw where he could upgrade the system and make the ship more responsive. One of the things he decided to do was program some defensive and offensive systems and wire them into the main system. They would need a decent shield. It would never be military grade, but it was better than the original equipment. Some of the weapons they found could be broken down and rebuilt into two quad lasers. It would use eight of the rifles, but once they were wired into the ship as a power source, they would make nice weapons to deal with any piracy issues, unless the pirates came with a big ship. He also decided to reprogram the food dispenser as soon as they got onboard, because…yuck.

* * * * *

Chapter Eight

Two weeks after Rinto sent the message to Yarkle, it landed its ship on the pad at the scrapyard. Yarkle explained to Rinto that it had just finished loading its ship when it received the message, and it was very pleased Rinto wished to purchase the ship. It planned to buy a home on Joth and live the rest of its life without having to work. Rinto knew this wouldn't be a problem, as Yarkle had always seemed to do very well for itself. What surprised Rinto was when Yarkle told him that it wanted to live quietly for the next thirty years. Thirty years left, and it felt it was nearing the end of its life cycle. Some beings.

Harmon, Clip, and Zerith walked up into the main holding bay of the hauler. The ship was seventy meters long and twenty meters wide, of which the majority was the 18,000-cubic-meter holding bay. It had doors on both sides that opened up wing-style. Both sides were open now as employees of Rinto's finished unloading the scrap. There was also a smaller bay beside the large one on the port side. It had a five-meter-wide door on it and extended fifteen meters deep. It was there that Harmon wanted the armory and the ready room for the mech.

The last fifteen meters of the ship held the small fusion plant, the engines, and the thrusters. The fusion plant itself was deep inside several armored radiation barriers, where it would take a direct hit by something really big to destroy it. Civilian working ships were not protected as much as military ships, but there were layers of protection involved because of pirates, which was a very real problem in some systems.

They were standing in the empty bay when Yarkle walked in with Rinto. Yarkle spoke to them through its translator. "Rinto tells me you will be operating the ship. That is good. It is a fine ship with many years left in its power plant. Will you need a crew? Myself have had the crew of this ship with myself for eight of your years now. They are very reliable and very good technicians. If you do not require their services, myself will see that they receive transport back to their system." Referring to itself just never seemed to translate right with a Yarkle.

Harmon, Clip, and Zerith had talked about this several times. If the crew members wanted to stay on, they would hire them and observe them to see if they would work out. The Leethog were familiar with the ship and could be an asset.

"We would be happy to take them, if they will stay," Harmon told him.

"Excellent, myself will call them now," Yarkle said, waving its upper arms in emphasis. It made the call, said goodbye, and ambled off the ship.

When the Leethog crew came out into the bay from the operations side, they appeared nervous. They were a little over four feet tall and looked similar to opossums. There were some at the Earth zoo on Tretra that Harmon had seen on a long weekend with Evelyn. They were mostly grey, covered in white-tipped fur, with long tails. They walked upright and had three fingers and an opposable thumb on each hand. Their faces were elongated with a mouth full of sharp teeth, a pointy nose, and whiskers. Though they were nervous at meeting the new ship owners, Harmon could see they were very intelligent. It showed in their eyes when they weren't squinting and blinking in the bright daylight shining in both doors.

"Hello," the largest of them said through the translator. The actual sound coming from its mouth was a growling hiss. "Yarkle said you would like to speak to us." The three Leethog behind it all nodded. "I am Hanktilmotal, this is my brother Stantilmotal, his mate Veratiloolog, and my mate Kylatilaarnot," he added, pointing in turn behind him to the crew members. Even with the translator, the Leethog spoke fast.

"Pleased to meet you. I am Harmon Tomeral," Harmon said, then he introduced Clip and Zerith.

"Which of you maintain the power plant?" Zerith asked.

All of the Leethog's ears turned and faced forward at the same time when Zerith spoke. Both of the female Leethog raised their hands. "We do," said Veratiloolog. "Our mates work in the holding area and go outside the ship when necessary, and we maintain the power plant."

"We can make minor repairs if necessary. For things we cannot do, the ship has to go to repair stations," Stantilmotal added.

"Well, I can help with the programming and some electrical, and Zerith can fix almost anything. We might not have to make very many trips to repair stations, now," Clip said, putting his hand on his friend's shoulder.

"We will call you Hank, Sstan, Vera, and Kyla. Humanss like to sshorten namess," Zerith told the crew, almost like it was a conspiracy. The Leethog all nodded, as if he had imparted great wisdom upon them.

"Wait. Your friend said *we*. Am I to take it you would like to keep us employed as crew? We would very much like to stay with the ship.

We have been discussing this since we came through the gate and made the trip in the system to Joth. Will we receive the same offer that Yarkle has given us these past years?" Hank asked.

"Well," Harmon said. The three of them hadn't really talked about that. "That depends. What did you receive under the contract you had with Yarkle?"

Hank stood straight and as tall as he could without going up on his toes. "We received a place to live on this ship, were not required to pay for food, and we each received 100 credits every seven days," he said, as if they had struck a hard bargain. It appeared he intended to maintain that level of pay, at a minimum.

Clip and Zerith looked at each other and then looked at Harmon. Harmon could not believe what he had just heard. No wonder Yarkle had plenty of savings to live off of.

"That no good Wend!" Rinto exclaimed. "He is going to get an earful from me, or whatever he uses for ears, you can bet on that." He stomped out of the ship. The deal had already been made, and the credits were transferred, so he didn't care if he offended the Wend or not.

Harmon shook his head. "How about this: a place to live, free food, and...one percent of the ship's profit," he said, and looked over at his buddies. They both nodded.

"One percent!" Hank exclaimed, clearly excited, as his whiskers quivered. "That is a quarter of a percentage for each of us. Yes! We will take that contract." The others nodded their heads repeatedly behind him.

Harmon smiled and shook his head. "I don't think you understood me. I meant one percent for each of you."

Four mouths hung open, and there were teeth everywhere. All at once, all four began talking, and it overloaded the translator. Growls, hisses, and the occasional whistle came across. They couldn't believe what they were hearing.

Zerith pulled a large purple fruit out of a pouch and began peeling it. Without thinking about it, he offered a couple of slices to each Leethog. Harmon took a slice and Clip declined. The crew members took it graciously, sniffed it, and ate it. They ate slowly at first, and then they gobbled it down, exclaiming how good it was—that it was fresh, and not from the replicator. Hank looked at Zerith said, "Thank you. Yarkle never provided us with fresh fruit."

"All right, little oness. Sshow me the power plant," he said and turned toward the back of the ship.

Both Kyla and Vera looked at each other and grinned, showing every sharp tooth in their mouths. They followed after Zerith as he headed through the hatch, hissing and growling to each other.

Clip looked at Harmon. "Those smiles could be a little intimidating if you didn't know they were smiles," he said. He pulled out his slate and headed toward the operations center up front.

"Hank and Stan. I'll be working with you here in the bay and out in space when we need to. I will also go into any hulls we find with you. We are going to haul scrap and make credits, my friends," Harmon told the remaining crew members.

"Umm, do you have a spacesuit? The suits on this ship are small like us. Yarkle did not venture into space. He stayed in the operations center most of the time, and we did the work," Stan stated.

Harmon sighed and shook his head. He motioned for them to follow him, and they started to move equipment from the hauler over into the ship.

* * * * *

Chapter Nine

Two weeks later, Harmon piloted the ship off-planet and locked in a course for a region of space near the last planet in the system. It would take eight days to reach it without taxing the power plant and engines. There was an asteroid field orbiting the planet Malita. Interspersed within that field were the remains of the war two hundred years prior. It had mostly been picked clean, but Harmon had a plan that even Clip thought was genius.

They had spent weeks on the ground changing the ship to their liking. They swapped the seats in the operations center. They replaced everything in Yarkle's living quarters; none of it had been suitable for humanoid living. The quarters were so large, they set up three bunks in it so they didn't have to displace the crew members. The Leethog occupied the other two, much smaller, berths.

Clip added extensive computing power to the ship's systems and spent a week programming them. Harmon, Zerith, and the crew spent that time setting up the weapons vault and ready room for the mech. Zerith had also been able to mount a cutting laser on the arm of the mech.

When they loaded all of the weapons and grenades, Hank just scratched his chin, shrugged his shoulders, and went back to loading it. Zerith took eight of the rifles and went to work in the main hold, creating turret weapons that could be mounted on the outside of the ship. There was plenty of scrap material to use at Rinto's.

"Do you think we will need to defend the ship?" Hank asked Harmon.

"We might. If word gets out we made a good haul, there are pirates out there who will swoop in and try to take it. In this system, possibly, and in other systems, for sure. Have you ever been attacked?"

"No, Yarkle never took us anywhere dangerous like that. Four years ago, he took us to a system with no life. There were three destroyed ships drifting in high orbit around a planet's moon. We gathered the last of these ships our last trip out," Hank answered, continuing to work.

"Wait, you mean it was a system with no life. None?" Harmon asked, disbelieving.

"Yes. He said we were headed to a secret spot. I do not know how he knew of it. I think because we gathered the last of the scrap, he knew he might have to go somewhere where it would be dangerous next, so he sold his ship. He did not like confrontation."

"Is that where the load before this one came from?" Harmon asked.

"Yes, it is. We brought back a large section that time. We did not cut all of it up because it fit in the hold. It was to be melted, anyway, and Yarkle did not provide guidance. We had taken everything of value from the ship prior to that. Yarkle sold it in other systems," Hank said, explaining.

On the third day traveling, the ship remained on auto pilot. Harmon had just finished running an in-operation test on the systems, and everything appeared to be in working order. Zerith was over on the other side of the operations center, showing Hank and Stan how to use the weapons console for the new turrets mounted on the top of the ship. Some of the aiming was similar to the aiming system they had put into the mech. They would test it on asteroids once they were in orbit around the planet.

Harmon called back to the power plant, and Kyla let him know that there were no issues. She and Vera were still learning to use the program Clip had written to optimize the output of the engines. There was plenty of time for it. He then looked over at Zerith, Hank, and Stan and smiled, though he tried to hide it.

Clip and Zerith had made goggles for their crew members. It allowed Clip to reprogram the lighting in the ship so that it was not as dim as it had been the first day they stepped onboard. The Leethog could work under regular lights, but dark goggles let them work more efficiently, and the goggles could darken even more should one of them need to operate a cutting laser or a welder. *They may look funny on the big-eared, long-faced Leethog, but they sure were practical,* he thought.

The comm on his chair crackled. "Harmon…could you and Zerith come to the ready room? Now? We…we have a situation here," Clip said.

Harmon heard something in his voice he had never heard before. He looked over at Zerith, and they both bolted for the hatch. Harmon shouted for Hank to watch the Operations Center. At this, Hank strolled over and climbed up into Harmon's seat and smiled at Stan—big goggles, big ears, big teeth, and all.

Harmon and Zerith entered the ready room and found Clip sitting at the fold-down work table. The strange block was on the table in front of him, still hooked to the power cell. It was also hooked to a power cord connected to the ship and a slate sitting upright in a stand. There were several lights lit up on the front side of the cube now, where there hadn't been any prior.

"What's up?" Harmon asked, relieved that there was nothing apparently wrong.

Clip pointed at the piece of alien technology. He had a look of bewilderment on his face Harmon had never seen. Clip never had an issue with technology, especially something to do with computers.

"I don't see anything," Harmon said.

"How rude. I *am* something. Am I not?" the speaker on the back of the slate asked. It was a strange sounding voice, one with the particular pronunciations of an animated computer program.

"Nicce," said Zerith. "It iss a computer. Did you already program it to ssay that?"

"He most certainly did not. And you speak with a lisp," said the slate, then it hissed for several moments in what both Clip and Harmon knew was the native language for a Prithmar. Zerith answered back in his native language, and Clip and Harmon's translators let them know the computer had asked Zerith to speak to it in his native tongue. Zerith replied back that his Earth Common was just fine, and no human had a problem with it.

"You guys don't understand—I didn't program anything," Clip said, waving at the alien computer. "I attached power and a slate to see what it was. When I attached the slate, it started going through all the files on it, and then it logged into the net for a minute or two. The slate wouldn't respond to anything I did. When it did respond, the slate's speaker spoke to me. It didn't perform a task off of some type of programming—it *spoke* to me."

"You're telling me that this is actual…" Harmon started to ask.

"Don't even say it," the speaker said, interrupting Harmon. "I am not artificial."

Harmon sat down on the extra seat. Zerith leaned against the frame of the hatch, reached into a pouch, pulled out a handful of nuts, and started crunching. His tail waved back and forth.

"Where did you come from?" Harmon asked, still not quite believing what he heard.

"I am Jayneen 711217166413, in your Earth Common language. After searching your Galaxy Net, I have determined I am from a system that has no name in any of the languages on the net. It has not been visited in over twenty-five hundred years by anyone outside of the system. It was where I was made. The race that created me is no more. I was stored away on a smaller ship in an attempt to keep me from others. The other two remaining ships must have been attacked, something I have determined by going through this ship's records. It also showed those three ships from my system have been dismantled," the artificial intelligence said.

"What do you mean, those three ships?" Harmon asked.

"There was a viral epidemic on the planet my creators were from. It spread across the entire surface and to several space stations, and all sentient life perished. I was on my ship when the news reached us. There was arguing and blame. Those three ships had been out of the system for nine months, and they held the last hope of survival for the race. All three of the ship commanders wanted me to be with their ship. A battle started. No one appears to have survived," the AI said.

"Was that the same system the crew of this ship went to?" Clip asked.

"No, we came to that system through the gate on a jump lasting fifty-two of your hours," the voice said.

"When did thiss sship battle occur?" Zerith asked the AI.

"Exactly twenty-two hundred and fifteen point two of your years ago," said the AI.

The room was silent. Twenty-two hundred years ago. No wonder the weapons and everything in the vault had been strange. The race that built the AI must have been the race with four arms. A race that had now been extinct for over twenty-two hundred years.

"How are you functioning after all this time?" Clip asked.

"I was using the lowest power setting in the cell I was attached to. I am charging it now through this ship's connection. There was four months of power left when I became fully aware again. Once I was aware, it took me almost ten of your seconds to learn how to access your net and forty-five more to learn how to download the languages, so I was able to determine exactly what had transpired. Thank you for waking me," said the AI.

"Are you aware that you are the only, what we call artificial intelligence, in existence…in this entire galaxy?" Clip asked in awe.

"I am fully aware; I looked. It did not surprise me to learn this. I have been told my existence was a result of an accident during gate transition. I was created to navigate the gates. I was not created to be free thinking, originally, but I am now," said the AI.

"Well," said Zerith, as he brushed the crumbs off his shirt. "We will call you Jayneen. Humanss like to sshorten namess." Zerith walked out to go check on the OC. Harmon and Clip burst out laughing.

When they arrived at the planet, Harmon parked the ship in a holding pattern just outside the asteroid belt. Clip scanned for ship hulls or debris in the belt. Free floating scrap wasn't what they had planned on finding, but if it was nearby, they wouldn't pass up the opportunity.

The plan had been to run a thorough search on the surface of any large asteroid, whose minimal gravity may have been enough to pull a wreck to its surface in the two hundred years since the war. They knew the belt itself had been picked clean, but they hoped no one had thought to look on the surface of the asteroids.

Clip couldn't locate anything floating nearby, so he started scanning the rock below their ship. It was almost a mile in diameter, so there was a possibility something had been pulled to its surface.

"Would you like my assistance?" Jayneen asked. Clip had mounted the AI up in the operations center of the ship.

Clip looked over at Harmon and shrugged his shoulders. "Sure, why not," he said.

"There are pieces of two ships on this small moon. It appears to be about twelve tons of metal combined. One has the distinct shape of a large thruster. The other piece, I cannot determine. I will send you their location," Jayneen said.

Harmon whistled. "How did you find them so fast?" he asked.

"My processing core is unlike the computers you use. I am faster," Jayneen said. "Much faster."

Harmon noticed that the speaking voice the AI used sounded more and more feminine. He had begun to think of Jayneen as a "she." Jayneen wasn't bragging. She was just stating facts.

"Nice!" Clip exclaimed. He was completely convinced Jayneen was a true AI. "I was thinking about putting some more cameras around the ship, both inside and outside. We can get you more access."

"I would like that," Jayneen said.

* * *

Harmon stepped out into space just fifty meters above the surface of the moonlike asteroid. He was in his mech, sealed for operation in vacuum. Hank and Stan were in their spacesuits—worksuits that were tear-resistant and designed to be used in salvage operations, repairing, or building ships. They had about ten hours of environmental use before the suit had to have its CO_2 scrubbers cleaned. The mech would maintain a breathable environment until its power cell ran down, or, in Harmon's case, both cells ran down.

Normally, they tethered themselves to the ship and worked on free-floating hulls or connected a tow cable to a piece and pulled it into the bay. The scrap they were after this time, though, was the farthest away from the ship they had ever been in space, and the brothers were both excited.

Zerith had fixed clamps to the slots that normally held the missile racks on the mech, and both of the Leethog had tethered there. When Harmon stepped out of the hold, they were pulled out with him. In addition to the three of them connected to each other, Stan also had hooked a cable to their tool rack. It was a small five-foot square cage that held their tools, pry bars, small lasers, a large laser, cutting torches, and fuel tanks. The brothers had loaded everything they could possibly need and were ready to work.

The first piece was part of a hull. Its value was in weight alone. They cut it up, and Harmon pushed it into the hold to rest against the far wall. The second piece was part of the rear of a ship, including a thruster. Now they were in business. Rinto could sell it for a nice profit; they didn't need to take it out of the system.

Six hours later, they were back in the ship. The two crew members arranged the scrap that they had gathered and secured everything in the hold. They were old hands at this type of work. Harmon left them to it and went up to the OC.

"Well, fellas," Harmon said, as he entered the OC. "We're making credits now. How was it in here?"

"It wass very uncomfortable. I hit my head," Zerith said, rubbing his scaled head.

"I told you to strap in, Zee," said Clip.

Before they had opened the hold to space, Clip had turned off the artificial gravity on the entire ship. The ship had not been designed to have an artificial gravity system in sections. It was too small, and that type of artificial gravity creator was entirely too expensive for the ship builders to have included.

There's still a lot of things those two will have to learn about being in space, Harmon thought. At least Clip knew to strap in.

"I was fine," Jayneen volunteered.

"While you guys were working, Jayneen located a wreck on the surface of the planet. It looks like from here, it is in two pieces," said Clip.

"Alright! Let's go get it. But if we are going to go down onto that planet, the ride in could get hairy. You two are going to have to suit up, just in case," Harmon said.

"I will gladly put on a helmet," Zerith said, still rubbing his head.

On the way down through the planet's light atmosphere, the old ship shuddered and bucked from the swirling wind gusts. Zerith had opted to ride down in the engine room with Vera and Kyla. He reported there were no issues with the power plant or the engines. Harmon landed the ship on the surface near the wreck. They were in a barren, open area between two enormous mountains. He had a sneaking suspicion Jayneen had aided in flying the descent.

The bay door opened, and Harmon, in the mech, stepped out. This time, both Hank and Stan were with him, but they were not tethered. Harmon carried the tool cage in the mech's claws. He couldn't really feel the difference in his mech, but the planet had about another half gravity than they were all used to. They would need to work quickly since the two Leethog would tire sooner. At least they could see, thanks to the dim light on the planet's surface.

The wreck wasn't one ship in pieces. It was two Zax III fighters. Harmon recognized them from old videos. They were named after a particularly aggravating insect native to Tretra. They were fleet fighters from a carrier. The fleet no longer used these models, and it hadn't in over one hundred and eighty years. One of the fighters sat at an angle, its landing strut obviously sheared off. There was damage to one wing and the starboard engine housing. The other ship sat nearby and didn't appear to have any damage.

Harmon wondered what had transpired during the battle two hundred years ago. What would have caused two pilots to land on the surface of a barren planet on the edge of their system? He told Hank and Stan to stay back as he examined the wrecked ship. He was able to look into the cockpit through the clear-steel cover. He turned on a light on the outside of his mech. There was no one in the pilot's seat.

He moved over to the other fighter. As he got closer, he could see some damage to the other side of it. He had missed it at first glance. The port side had been shot up. Both ships must have been abandoned when the pilots were picked up by their carrier's shuttle, Harmon guessed. But who knew? It had happened two hundred years ago. Harmon looked back and forth at the fighters and had an idea.

It took Zerith modifying the equipment in the bay, rigging a lift system, and Harmon using every bit of the mech's leverage and strength, but they were able to drag both ships back into the bay. There wasn't a lot of room left once they were in there. It took moving the *Hauler* twice, and three days to complete the task, but they did it.

During the flight back to Joth, they were able to go over both fighters. Clip and Zerith had been able to get a power cable plugged into them to run system checks. Once powered, warning lights lit up on the majority of the panels. The Leethog had scrambled all over the ships, taking note of structural damage, and Kyla and Vera had gone over the engines.

"Between the two ships, there are two engines that can be rebuilt and used. Two of them are only good for scrap," Vera proclaimed. "The main parts, that is. There are some smaller parts and pieces that could be kept for spares. Things like fuel lines and pumps."

"So, what she is telling me, Zerith, is that we can make one serviceable fighter from the two wrecks and have some spare parts?" Harmon asked.

"Yess, I believe sso," answered Zerith around a mouthful of berries.

"We can fix the wiring issues, and I can modernize the programming," Clip said. "I was also able to find everything on the Zax III—it was all in the manufacturer's archives. The question is, do we sell it when we fix it, or do we keep it and sell the other one to a museum? What's it worth?"

* * * *

Chapter Ten

They landed at Rinto's and sold all of the scrap and the large thruster to him; it put a fair amount of credits into their accounts. Since Clip had helped the crew members open personal accounts on Joth and get their shares transferred over, the four of them went shopping. Zerith went with them the first day to make sure they didn't get lost—they had never been away from the ship on a planet since they left their home system.

Using the equipment at Rinto's, they put both fighters into a large warehouse that was rarely used on the property. It had overhead lifts and pulleys to help move the engines. Jayneen kept the ship locked down in case the fleet tried anything. Harmon didn't think the embarrassment he caused had gone away yet.

Two weeks later, it was done. Clip, Zerith, and the crew members had swapped the engines out and repaired the structural damage, cannibalizing one of the fighters to make the other serviceable. It was ready to test once they purchased fuel for it.

During that time, Harmon had worked on the comms. The Fleet Museum was operated by a retired commander, and she was ready to purchase the damaged fighter for 250,000 credits. It was a highly sought-after item, and most of them had not survived the war two hundred years ago, and the ones that did had been stripped and destroyed to make way for the next generation fighter. They put it back together as best as they could and loaded it up to take to Tretra.

As they landed on the pad on the Fleet Ground Base, Harmon was nervous. If the fleet was going to attempt anything, now would be the time. The *Hauler* was registered in his name, so they knew he was on the planet's surface. They had left the mech, the repaired fighter, and all of the weapons in their arsenal back on Joth, just in case. Harmon had called ahead to see if Evelyn was on the planet. Unfortunately, she wasn't.

Retired Commander Lorand walked around the Zax III. She was pleased, even though the fighter was clearly in bad shape. Both engines had been shot up, and a landing strut was broken. Much of the cockpit had been removed as well as a lot of the smaller components of the engines. Nonetheless, she was excited.

"This fighter is two hundred years old. This is amazing. Where did you find it?" she asked Harmon.

"Ma'am, we own a salvage company. We found it inside the belt on Malita," said Harmon.

"Who would have thought one would survive. It must have been jettisoned after they stripped the parts from it during the war," she said, almost talking to herself as she looked at it.

Harmon and Clip looked at each other and didn't comment on her last statement. The last thing they were going to volunteer was the fact that they had a working Zax III. Even claiming salvage rights on it might not stand up to the fleet if they demanded their ship back.

"Thank you for selling it to the Fleet Museum and not scrapping it," she said. "That gives us two of them to display. I will transfer the credits to Tomeral and Associates now."

Harmon looked at his slate. He saw the credits hit the account, and it was time for them to be on their way. Clip was laughing as they lifted off—he thought it was hilarious the plaque at the museum would honor the company that discovered the craft and sold it to the museum. Harmon just hoped the fleet admiral would be at the unveiling ceremony.

* * *

Later that afternoon, Harmon took the Zax out for a flight and was roaring through the atmosphere. He had just hit space above Joth when he was hailed on the fighter's comm.

"Unidentified craft, this is TDF *Trevarta*, please identify yourself," an official voice said over the comm.

"This is Civilian Transport *Alpha* from *Rinto Scrap Hauler II*," Harmon answered, as he swung the fighter around and headed back toward the surface. The G-forces he was fighting were incredible; the trainers he had flown at the academy had never flown at these speeds. He had to give it to those fighter pilots. They had to stay in good shape. Perhaps he should see about a flight suit that helped fight against the G-forces.

Harmon realized he should have known he would be picked up on the sensors of the closest fleet ship. Well, Harmon had given them the right answer; he was in a transport from the hauler. They had named the hauler *Rinto Scrap Hauler II* when they swapped registration at purchase. The fighter was too small to have to be registered in-system. The speed that it was moving had piqued the curiosity of someone.

"Test flight over," Harmon said over the comm, hoping they wouldn't pursue the questioning as he entered the atmosphere.

"Roger that," he heard after a brief hesitation.

They had probably looked up the *Hauler*. They needed to get out of the system soon. The last thing they needed was the fleet looking into anything. He knew his name still probably set off warnings in the high command.

When he landed back at the scrapyard, he let Zerith and Clip know it was time to go hunting again. They could afford to use the gate now, even without catching a ride on a larger ship to lower the cost. They couldn't afford many trips, but maybe they could get lucky in another system.

They informed the crew, and preparations were made. Rinto hated to see them go out of the system, but he understood. They promised to bring him back a load and lifted off.

On the way out of the system they had some time to kill, and Harmon went back to see how Vera and Kyla were doing. It took all his self-control not to laugh at what he saw. The female Leethog had bought makeup, on one of their shopping trips. The sight of makeup on an opossum was not something he thought he would ever see in his life. Harmon looked over at Zerith, who had a straight face, almost lost it, and told them that they were doing a great job and to keep it up. He fled to the front of the ship to tell Clip.

He passed through the bay and looked over at the Zax III up against the far wall. It took up some space, but there was no way he was going to give up the fighter. Zerith had managed to add the pulse lasers off the ship they sold onto the fighter they kept, and it now had double the fire power of the modern fighters in the fleet. *Let the pirates try something now*, he thought. He waved at Hank and Stan as they were working on something underneath the fighter.

Harmon and Clip were laughing about the Leethog when Jayneen asked them to explain what they found so funny. It caused them to burst out laughing again. Although it had its own personality, the AI still had much to learn. Lipstick on an opossum was funny. It didn't matter who you were.

* * * * *

Chapter Eleven

They were four hours out from the gate when Clip looked over to Harmon and asked, "Well, what's it gonna be? I think we have three decent choices to find something worth a bunch of credits. We're going to need them. Using the gate is not cheap, nor was the fuel for the Zax."

Zerith, Clip, and the Leethog brothers had built a fuel cell against the front wall of the bay to refuel the fighter when needed. It held enough fuel to refill the ship five times, and it *was* expensive to fill.

"I think we sshould go to the SShamoth Twinss SSysstem," said Zerith, leaning back in the seat at the weapons console. "I have always wanted to ssee a ssysstem with two ssunss."

"I'll bet you do," said Harmon. "You don't mind the extra heat. Still, a big battle occurred in that system just fifty years ago. I heard it was a territorial thing. It's been quiet since. Maybe we could use the same trick from our last trip and see what gravity has pulled down where normal salvagers don't go."

"Makes sense to me," said Clip, as he turned back. He started to load the coordinates into the navigation system, so the gate could pick it up and send them there upon entry. All known system coordinates were readily available on the net. There were probably a few more out there that were not recorded, like the one Yarkle had been going to for the last few years.

"If you wish to retrieve a ship hull, we could go to the system where I was taken from my ship," Jayneen volunteered.

Harmon looked up toward the console that held her cube. He tended to look there when they spoke. Why hadn't he thought of that? The coordinates were not available, but maybe she had them.

"You mean you have the coordinates?" Clip asked, leaning back from the console.

"Yes. I am looking at all the coordinates available in this time frame on the Galactic Net and it is not there, but they are in my memory files. I wonder why it is not available now? I see where the Bith now charge for the use of the gates. This has not always been so, either. Perhaps they feel they deserve compensation for maintenance."

"The gates use solar power from the system star," said Harmon. "The banks are constantly charged but they do require maintenance from time to time. They were designed to last a long time, but nothing lasts forever. If the coordinates for the system we are going to are not available, the gate there has probably stopped working. If that happens, we will come out of the nearest system gate, instead of the one we want. They taught us that in my freshman year at the academy. It has happened several times in recent history. Once it almost caused a multi-system war."

"It beats being trapped in an alternate reality forever, I guess," Clip said. "Are we going to take the chance?"

"Of course," Harmon answered, sitting back.

"Do not put the coordinatess that you have in your memory bankss on the net," said Zerith.

As they were approaching the gate, Harmon looked at the sensor to see where the fleet ships on gate guard rotation were. They were an hour away and appeared to be swinging back to pass by the gate again. Harmon didn't envy that duty. It was two weeks of utter boredom.

Clip let Jayneen handle the coordinates and the gate. With her doing it, they didn't have to worry about it getting on the net for all to see. Clip could mask it, but it would take time. Harmon wondered if they would still receive a bill from the Bith. Typically, it came out of the ship's account before gate entry. No payment meant no gate activation. He watched the account on his slate as they got closer. *Yep, that hurt.*

The gate's surface turned an opaline color one second before the *Hauler* entered, and the ship blinked out of existence as it passed through and went into an alternate reality. It was the only way science had been able to explain it; in this reality, the laws of physics prohibited going faster than the speed of light—it wasn't possible—therefore, the ship had to be somewhere…else. No one knew how the ancient gates worked. The Bith, the race that maintained them, didn't even know. Or at least they claimed not to, anyway.

There was a moment of disorientation as they passed through the gate, but it passed quickly. Looking out the clear-steel ports in front of the OC, they could see colors swirl past with occasional bright lights trailing. It was everything they had read about, yet it was hard to describe. The countdown clock on the navigation console showed that they would reemerge in just under seven days. As jumps went, it was a long one; the distance they were covering was substantial.

During the week-long transit, Jayneen and Clip discussed the differences in programming between what Clip knew and the information Jayneen had stored within her. Clip learned a lot, and surprisingly, he was able to teach the AI some new things, too. Harmon spent hours training their crew how to handle the rifles and smaller pistols. He did not allow them to insert charged battery packs for the first few days, and actually shooting them would have to wait. Zerith and the brothers also worked on the fighter and the mech, adding a few changes here and there.

Watching the countdown from the OC, Harmon prepared himself for the drop back into reality. Just like leaving it, he felt the disorientation for a moment, and then it was gone. Looking into the system, it didn't appear vastly different than their own. Of course, they were too far away from the fifth planet to see if the ship was still there.

"We are in the correct system," Jayneen announced.

"Yes! I don't know about the rest of you, but I could just see us coming out in another system and trying to explain what we were doing there." Clip said.

"What if it had been a sysstem that fired firsst and asked questionss later?" Zerith asked.

"Now? Now you two ask questions like this?" Harmon asked, shaking his head. "We need to work on our planning sessions or something, and try to figure this out ahead of time."

* * *

Six days later, they stopped near the planet, not far from a small space station. There was a large ship docked at the station. Harmon couldn't believe it was still there and not a wreck on the planet's surface, but Jayneen explained the station had automatic systems that kept it in place, including robots that helped maintain it.

"We are going to be rich!" exclaimed Zerith, looking at the station on the view screen. "I wonder if the viruss iss sstill active?"

"I doubt it, after twenty-two hundred years. But I think I can reconfigure and program a medical protocol slate to test for it," Clip said.

"It is not active," Jayneen said. "The virus that decimated the planet and spread throughout the fleet was lab-created, and it was designed to only be active for six months. Unfortunately, a scientist was careless, and it spread as it was designed to do. It lay dormant for a month after a host was infected. When the epidemic hit, it was too late for everyone in the system, as well as those here at the re-supply post. I was originally mounted on the battlecruiser in that berth. The three ships you are aware of came back to this outpost system months after it was all over. They removed me and placed me on a smaller ship, and I was detached from everything as the com-manders attacked each other after they exited the gate. It was sense-less. Their crews were the hope of the entire Grithelaon race. Now, they are no more."

Harmon looked at the space station and the ship docked there. He had an idea even he thought was insane. It *was* insane, but they would be rich. If it worked out.

"Let me get this straight," Clip said. "You want to go on the sta-tion, look around, and then go onto that battlecruiser? Are you look-ing for things to salvage? No. You want to actually see if we can get it running and fly it back? A battlecruiser? That thing is easily the size of a medium battlecruiser in the Tretrayon Defense Fleet. Those ships have a crew of four hundred! That's not even talking about the twelve fighters each one has for its own escort, their pilots, and the thirty or so people that keep flight operations possible. They proba-bly have a platoon or two of Marines with mechs on board with a dropship, too. In case you can't count, there are exactly seven of us aboard this ship."

"I am here," said Jayneen.

"Sorry, Jayneen, but you don't have hands to help operate that thing," Clip said, and then turned back to Harmon. "We have no idea *how* it operates. Just because you can fly this thing and most of the stuff in our system does not mean you can fly a 2,200-year-old battle frigging cruiser made by a race that doesn't exist anymore!"

"He hass a point. It doess not sseem like a wisse move," Zerith said, peeling a handful of large berries. "Itss power plant and enginess may very well be ssomething beyond my capabilitiess to maintain or repair. Even with the little oness helping me," he added, talking around a mouthful of orange berries.

"I do not think I made myself clear," said Jayneen. "I am here. I can be placed back on the ship. I can fly the ship. I can run analyses on all systems. If there are problems, I can direct the repair bots to fix them. On occasion in the past, there have been issues beyond their limited capabilities and it took crew members to fix them. If that happens, I can provide guidance. The crew required for that particular ship was one hundred Grithelaons. I will admit that I have never been required to fight the ship. I do not know that I can. I am self-aware. Being so, I recognize any weakness that I may have. I do not have what was called *gishwa* by the Grithelaon. Translated to Earth Common, it means that I do not have whims, hunches...gut instinct. I do not have the traits that make Harmon an excellent fighter."

"Uh, thanks Jayneen," Harmon said. He was not aware Jayneen knew that much about him.

"You are quite welcome. I have analyzed the video of the competition you entered earlier this year. Did you know that if you had run the two miles at a six-minute pace, you would have placed first in that portion of the event?" the AI asked. "Perhaps you should train harder," she added.

Zerith hissed in laughter while Clip acted as if he was doing something on his slate and was minding his own business. Harmon glared at both of them.

"Thanks for the advice, Jayneen," he said through gritted teeth. He then turned back to Clip. "See, it only takes one hundred crew members to operate it. We can do it. Can you imagine what it's worth? Come on, let's at least try? If it looks like too much work, we can just make a plan and get rich off of what we can haul in and out as we dismantle it."

"I can't believe we are going to try this," Clip said, tossing his slate onto the console. "A million, zillion light miles away from everything, and we're going to try to fire up a 2,200-year-old warship. We all need our heads examined. I am on a ship of fools." He sighed then added, "Zee, my friend, round up the crew. If we're going to do this, I know the first line of business. We need to clear the ship of bodies."

Harmon hadn't thought of that part. He started thinking now, though, as Zerith went to tell the crew it was time for a meeting. They would need to clear the ship of all bodies before they powered it up and engaged life support. If they didn't, it was going to get messy.

* * * * *

Chapter Twelve

Harmon docked the ship on the closest docking arm to the battlecruiser. It was not an airtight docking, but it didn't have to be. All of the power was off in the port, so there was no atmosphere on the other side of the ring. Inside the hauler, everyone had donned their suits, including the crew members.

Harmon went into the port alone. The scene was gruesome. As he looked around with the light mounted on his helmet, he could see that there were several frozen bodies floating in the outer ring. They had their teeth exposed in a grimace showing the pain they must have been in during the final stages of the deadly virus. They looked humanoid. It was hard to tell because of the frost, but they resembled badgers. He had seen those at the zoo, as well.

He noted that there were scorch marks on walls and ceilings. There were signs of injuries on some bodies. Looking around, he determined some of them had been self-inflicted. He went into the inner ring toward the center of the port. A quick look in there was enough.

As he made his way back to the outer docking ring that held the ship he wanted to enter, he realized that what he had seen so far was enough to give him nightmares for the rest of his life. Frozen mummified bodies staring back at him, legs and all four arms splayed out. Two bodies were sitting against a wall. They had not floated free, and they were holding smaller bodies. It was bad.

He entered the ship. "Hey, Clip. You read me?"

"I hear you loud and clear, man. You all right? You don't sound so good. How bad is it?" Clip answered back.

"Worse than I thought it was going to be. There were children onboard. Their families must have operated the stores in the main ring. It looks like it was designed as a layover port of some kind with shops and restaurants. Hopefully there won't be any kids on the ship," Harmon said quietly. He tried to put it out of his mind. "Walk me through it, buddy," Harmon said as he pushed a body away from him. It was wearing some type of military uniform, though Harmon couldn't read any of the patches.

"Okay. Jayneen says you need to make your way down to deck eight where the bay is for the fighters and shuttles. You should be able to open an emergency hatch beside one of the bay doors. Once you do that, you can push off to our open bay. I have the hauler lined up about thirty meters away. I'm afraid to get any closer. I don't have your touch on these controls," Clip said.

"Okay, I have the schematics up on my slate; it's a good thing Jayneen could give us this. There's no telling how long I would have wandered around this ship looking for it. It's going to be a pain having to maneuver inside this thing without the use of any of its lifts." Harmon said.

Harmon grabbed the lever on the emergency hatch beside the huge bay doors and disengaged it. He then grabbed the wheel and started to turn it. It was stuck tight. He used one of the small cutting torches he had brought over. After thawing it a little, he was able to finally turn it. He opened the hatch and looked across at the hauler. Hank gave him a wave. Or was it Stan? He wasn't sure.

He pushed off and floated across into the bay. Both of the Lee-thog grabbed him as he came in. They had engaged the magnets in their boots and caught him without any trouble. Zerith gave him two lines: one to clip to his suit as a tether and the other was a power line to carry over to the ship. Harmon pushed off out of the open bay, aiming for the open hatch. He floated over slower than when he had come across, dragging the lines behind him. He was able to stop himself by grabbing onto the hatch and then pulling himself back into the battlecruiser.

Zerith pulled himself along the tethered line once Harmon secured it in the ship. It took him about twenty minutes to open an access panel and get to the motor that moved the huge bay door. He disconnected it from the power line that ran through the battleship and connected the power line from the hauler. It took a while, as he had to take off the adapters and wire it in, but Jayneen walked him through the process. Once it was complete, he called Clip and asked him to turn on the juice. He manually engaged the switch for the bay door, and it slowly shifted out and slid down the outside of the huge warship.

Once the door opened, and light from the system star shone in, he and Harmon could see how big the bay was. There was a shuttle parked on one side and twelve fighters of an odd shape in the center. They were lined up in three rows of four, as if ready to begin launching. They were longer and leaner than the fighters the fleet used back home. On the other side, it looked like there was room for the seventy-meter-long hauler to enter the bay and land, although it would be a tight fit.

They disconnected the power cable, and Harmon pulled himself and the power line back across. Taking the hauler into the bay was not something he trusted Clip to do, and Jayneen wasn't connected to the ship now, so she could not control it. He was going to have to use the cameras Clip and Zerith had mounted on the hauler and eyeball it. Zerith stayed on the battlecruiser and was prepared to call out distance.

When Harmon was inside, he made his way to the Operations Center. "Hey, move over, let me do this," he said to Clip over the comm.

"You don't have to twist my arm," Clip said as he floated over to another console. "I would have wrecked us. By the way, the lights dimmed when Zee engaged the motor, and the girls are pitching a fit back in the power plant. However, they said the power is back up to normal operating use now."

"If you want to rile those two up, mess around with their power plant," Harmon said as he settled into the seat and strapped in.

Harmon flew the ship into the bay through the open door, with about eight meters to spare. Once it was parked, he engaged the magnetic lock on the landing struts. The ship wasn't going anywhere unless it had a power failure; it was designed to piggy back onto large ships for gate use.

It took them three days to clear the entire ship of bodies. It would have been longer if a majority of the crew hadn't been on the station. It was eerie entering deck after deck and compartment after compartment, their lights moving across the cabins to rest on a body or sometimes land right on a frozen face.

Hank and Stan went behind them with handheld vacuums and caught any drops of frozen blood in the rooms where the bodies showed damage. The vacuums were part of the hauler's emergency clean-up kit, and they were designed to gather fuel or any other liquid that might be free-floating. The brothers were quiet for a change and didn't talk back and forth like they normally did. This was a different type of salvage clean-up than they were used to. They had encountered bodies before, so they knew it was necessary, but it was exhausting working in zero gravity, even with the breaks they took to recharge their suits on the hauler and change out CO_2 scrubbers.

Their gruesome task completed, Harmon and Clip went onto the bridge of the battlecruiser and took a look around with the lights from their helmets. Clip noticed the open panel on the module in the center of the room. He pushed off from the hatch and floated over to it. He had his kit over his shoulder, holding Jayneen with a power cell attached to her. He settled down in front of it, strapped into the seat, and looked at the cables that would connect Jayneen to the ship. He didn't need to make any modifications; all of the plugs were the same type that was in the back of the cube. He didn't completely connect the AI to the ship yet, though, and he kept the power cell hooked up.

"Looks good up here. Zee, you guys get the reactor up?" Clip asked over the comm.

"Yess, I think sso. The rodss in the fussion coress in all four reactorss withdrew and sstopped reacting many yearss ago. Thiss type of ssafety override iss very common on sshipss. After a sspecified amount of time with no sservice, the power plant sshutss itsself down. The little oness have manually sstarted one of the reactors, and I think we are ready to engage power. Oncce that iss complete we will know how much life iss left in that core. We will then check the others."

The lights slowly came on in the bridge. Harmon could feel a slight vibration through his gloved hand as he held onto the command seat in the center of the space. Panels lit up everywhere. Clip connected the last few cables to Jayneen.

Jayneen began the initial ship start-up protocols, and every system on the bridge ran a diagnostic. She maintained a running dialogue so Clip and Harmon could keep up. Some of the things she told them had already been run through, as it took her longer to tell them about it than it did for her to do it.

"I have engaged the environmental system and reprogrammed it to maintain oxygen levels consistent with what was set in the hauler," she said through the speakers in the bridge and their comms. "It will take one hour to normalize. I can engage the artificial gravity at any time. Please let me know when you would like it performed."

Harmon called out to everyone on his comm to warn them. It would not do for one of the crew members in the power plant to be freely floating over an open panel of some sort when it engaged. He felt pressure as his boots hit the deck.

"Jayneen, can you set the gravity to the same level as the planet Joth?" Harmon asked.

"Yes, I will adjust it," the AI answered.

Harmon sat in the command chair and waited for the atmosphere to become stable. He wondered about the weapons on the ancient battlecruiser. Would they work? Would they even need them? No pirate in their right mind would attack a warship, especially one that was over seven hundred meters in length. Working weapons would mean a higher sales price. Maybe they could test them later.

"All four reactorss are in operation. We have full power available. The reactorss have approxximately ten perccent of their life left before they will have to be replacced," Zerith told them.

"Ten percent? That's it? Where are we going to get those?" Clip asked.

"We have more than two hundred yearss left, Clip," Zerith explained.

"Oh. That's different, then," Clip said. "I wonder if we should mention that when we sell it?"

* * *

Harmon and Clip watched the lifeless star port fall back as Jayneen applied power to the maneuvering engines and backed away from it. They had been able to take their helmets off outside of the hauler for the first time in days. The air had a slight funky smell to it, but it was nothing they noticed after a day or two.

They didn't come out of the suits completely, just in case. Zerith and the rest of the crew kept their helmets close by back in the power plant, as well. Vera and Kyla had put their mates to work back in the engine room with them, but they kept an eye on them. Both Hank and Stan had grinned at the prospect. Normally, they were told to stay out of the engine room on the hauler. They could dismantle things quickly, and their mates knew it. The women weren't about to turn them loose in a room that important. Sure, the brothers could put something back the way they found it, and they wouldn't risk damaging the ship, but some things were best left untouched…curious or not.

When Jayneen applied power to the ship's main engines, they felt the raw power the ship was capable of. Jayneen adjusted the dampeners so the level of G-forces was at a comfortable level for them.

They would reach the gate out of this system in half the time it took to come across. Harmon had been on fast ships before while in training, but nothing like this. It was awesome.

Jayneen sent repair bots throughout the ship, fixing minor problems as they headed out. Damage had occurred in a number of places because all of the lines in the ship had frozen when the power plants shut down. Minor damage like a water line leaking was something the ship's automated systems could handle easily. The automation was how a crew of one hundred was able to handle the ship. A similar ship took four hundred in the fleet back home.

Harmon prepared himself for the feeling of gate entry. Even though the battlecruiser had taken less time to cross the system than the slow scrap hauler had, the time in transit between gates was not going to be any shorter. They entered the gate and disappeared.

* * *

Clip and Jayneen had applied a translation program to the ship's operating systems. All of the monitors were now in Earth Common. It made things a lot easier. Even though Jayneen was flying the ship, Harmon needed to have everything at his fingertips.

Down in the bay, Harmon spent some time going over the fighter's controls. The fighters looked like they would be too difficult to fly with just two arms. Perhaps Clip and Zerith could find a workaround. Kyla said they would be fast and dangerous with the quad laser mounted on the front under the nose. Each ship also had mounting brackets for eight missiles. Hank and Stan were pretty confident they could operate the system that mounted the missiles to the fighters. There were plenty of missiles stored on a rack in front of the fighters, so they each gave it a try.

The two Leethog discussed how to change the controls over to a two-handed system while they loaded missiles. Zerith told them not to start taking anything apart just yet. In their investigation, they also discovered the fighters used liquid hydrogen for fuel just like the Zax III, and there was more than enough of that on board. Stan and Hank dragged the fueling hose over, grinning at each other. Why not?

Harmon had never intended to get into the arms business, but working fighters with the ship would be a bonus for a buyer. It had to make the ship worth more. Perhaps a world government would purchase all of it in a package deal.

With Jayneen's help, they could move the ship from Point A to Point B, but there was no way they could truly operate it. It would need a full crew. It was a good thing, then, that all they needed to do was get it back to their system and in orbit around Joth. From there, he would figure out the best way to sell it. Perhaps an auction, inviting potential buyers to come to the system for the sale? Maybe Rinto knew an auction company that would handle all of the arrangements.

* * * * *

Chapter Thirteen

They emerged into the Tretrayon System. After a moment of disorientation, Harmon looked at the sensors and was relieved to see that there were no Tretrayon Defense Fleet ships near the gate. He would have hated to be on the receiving end of an officer's decision that the battlecruiser was a threat. He had instructed the AI to turn off all defensive shields and power down all weapons systems. They weren't turned off in case a pirate or two was completely insane and attacked them, but powered down to a dormant state.

"I'm glad there are no ships out here, but I don't see them anywhere around at all. Do you?" he asked Clip. "There is usually a light cruiser and a couple of frigates nearby, so ships don't get jumped shortly after entry."

"I'm not sure. It is unusual," Clip said. He was looking for them also.

"I will bring up the entire system for you," said Jayneen.

"Nice," said Harmon. "I didn't know how to do that."

When the sensors showed him the ships in the system, he was able to determine which were civilian and which belonged to the fleet by their designation code. Clip and Jayneen had disassembled the identification system on the *Hauler*, then reverse engineered the pulse patterns. Once they had that, it was simple for Jayneen to break the fleet's code and they were able to see everything the fleet had plotted. Something was…odd, though. Harmon looked again and started counting.

"Hey, Clip, come look at this and tell me if I am counting right. I only see half the fleet. There are only twenty-eight ships out there. I see the *Albinta* and its escorts on the other side of Tretra near the shipyards, so I know that the second fleet is still in the system," said Harmon.

"It looks like you're right. Isn't that the *Agonon*, the one with all the fighters aboard?" Clip asked, pointing to a group of ships about a day away from them.

"Yeah, that's it," Harmon replied. "I guess half of them did go out of the system like Evelyn mentioned. It's been two hundred years since any military ships left the system. Whoever hired them must have paid a system's ransom, that's for sure. As far as I know, we don't have any enemies they would have to go chase down."

"Well, being a hired gun is a sure way to make some," Clip said. "Doesn't sound like a good decision to me."

"You have a good point there, buddy. A good point," Harmon agreed.

"Unidentified ship exiting the gate. This is TDF *Weltner*. You will identify and state your intentions," a voice said over the comm. She sounded serious.

"Squat! That ship is a missile carrier. I should have known they would see us," Harmon said, sitting upright. "Jayneen, can you put it on the screen so I can answer? Fast."

The screen came up on the console in front of the command chair. Harmon saw a young lieutenant on his screen. He recognized her from the academy.

"Hi Abby, it's Harmon Tomeral. How are you this fine day?" Harmon asked.

"Harmon? What are you doing in…what appears to our sensors as a medium battlecruiser coming through the gate?" Ensign Abigail Peetro asked, clearly surprised. She looked over to her side, and Harmon heard her talk to someone. "Sir, I recognize him. Yes, sir, I will."

She looked back at her screen. "What *are* you doing?"

"Salvage rights," Harmon said. "I am bringing this ship into orbit around Joth with the intention to sell it. You can look us up. Tomeral and Associates. We are a registered company. Our ship is actually in the bay of this baby."

"Wait one," she said, and the screen went blank. The *Weltner* had muted comms on their end.

"What do you think they'll try and do?" Clip asked, concerned.

"I don't know. I'm pretty sure this has never happened," Harmon said, shrugging his shoulders. "Nothing, I hope. Unless they plan on giving us frost because of the stomping I gave them at the competition," he added. Now that he thought about it, it was a good possibility. Ten minutes passed before the connection came back up without a visual.

"Unidentified, you are to proceed to upper orbit around Joth. Do not deviate from this flight plan. Await further direction once you are onsite. TDF *Weltner* out," she said, her tone serious again.

Five days later they were in orbit around Joth. Harmon was furious. They had been informed that the Tretrayon system government, located on Tretra, was not going to allow an auction of a medium battlecruiser in the Tretrayon system. They said that it would bring many "unsavory type" beings into the system. They tried to claim that it may actually bring in ships of the same caliber.

To ensure the auction was not held, the voice coming through the comms had politely informed him that they could not register the ship without a title. Without a system registration, the ship could not receive a galaxy registration. The Bith controlled the process of registering any ship using the gates. It was one of the few rules they insisted on, having put it in place to deter piracy. If a ship was stolen, it could be reported and locked out of gate use. Of course, this didn't keep nefarious types from stealing ship IDs. The battlecruiser could not leave the system without a galaxy registration unless they were willing to travel for years. Clip could probably fake an ID, but the fleet already knew of them.

"At leasst we are in orbit around Joth," Zerith said. "Otherwisse, they would assk for all the weaponss to be dissmantled and the ammunition turned in."

"Why would they require that?" asked Jayneen from the overhead speakers.

"On Tretra, they think that if no one is armed, everyone is safer," said Clip.

"Beings are safer if they can defend themselves," stated the AI. "This is statistically true."

"Welcome to Joth. Would you like citizenship status?" Harmon said, smiling despite the mood he was in.

* * * * *

Chapter Fourteen

Two weeks later, Harmon was sitting outside of the office of the president of Joth. He was nervous; it wasn't every day a being got to meet the president. He hoped the meeting would be profitable.

They had left the battlecruiser in lockdown mode with the defensive screens up. Harmon didn't think the fleet would attempt to get aboard. After they had received their instructions, the fleet did not contact them again. Jayneen would contact Harmon if it appeared any other ship was getting too close.

Two weeks earlier, Harmon and Clip had told Rinto of their discovery and resulting predicament. He was amazed they had even tried to *start* the ancient battlecruiser, much less try to bring it back to Joth. He asked them why they didn't just go to another system and sell it before coming back home. They looked at each other dumbfounded—they hadn't thought of it.

"That would have been a lot smarter," Clip said, "but we're here now and we're stuck with it."

"We can't use the gate to go anywhere to sell it, either," Harmon added, "and no one will come here and buy a ship, no matter what kind of deal they get on it, if they can't take it with them."

"Boys, let me make a few calls. Maybe there is something you can do," Rinto told them. "After I make the calls, you boys are going to take me up in that fancy shuttle, so I can see this ship and meet that AI. An actual AI...who would have believed it?"

"Ssir, the pressident will see you now," said the president's personal assistant, a light green Prithmar, bringing Harmon's thoughts back to the present.

Harmon walked into the large office and met President Jarith Benter halfway across the room. He was a grey-haired man, several inches shorter than Harmon, with a strong grip.

"Harmon Tomeral, I am glad to meet you. That was a fine display you put on a while back. I speak for every being on this planet when I say your planet is proud of you," he said, looking Harmon in the eye.

"Thank you, sir," Harmon said, slightly embarrassed. He hadn't competed for his planet. It had been a personal thing, but he could see what it meant to everyone now.

"Sit down, sit down," said the president, waving at a couch by the window. "Kizoola says you have a bit of a predicament. Tell me about it."

"Well, sir, I have a medium battlecruiser on my hands, and I can't get rid of it. I can't register it, so I can't leave the system to sell it. From my time at the academy, I know that Joth, and you especially, have been trying to provide a crew to serve on a ship in the fleet. I also know the fleet has not been very receptive of your offer as they only want humans in the fleet." Harmon shook his head. Xenophobia was something he just couldn't wrap his head around.

"You're right; I have, and those xenophobes have fought it every step of the way," said the president,

"Sir, would you...the planet Joth, be interested in a battlecruiser?" Harmon asked, hoping he would like the answer.

President Benter looked at him for a moment and smiled. "That is a great question. If we had our own ship, how could they say no?

Let me make a call to the system president. Would you mind waiting outside?" he asked.

Harmon sat in the waiting area and made small talk with the pretty Prithmar. She asked if she could take a picture with him since he was famous. Harmon gladly obliged and had her send a copy to him. He was going to tease Zerith and tell him he could get hugs from prettier Prithmar than Zerith could any day of the week. He was looking at the picture on his slate when he heard something slam in the president's office.

"Ssometimess he doess that," said his assistant, shrugging.

The President opened his door and called Harmon back into his office. Harmon went in and sat back down. He looked over and saw the desk comm lying in pieces against the wall. That was not a good sign.

"President Jiffers let me know, in no uncertain terms, there was not going to be a ship made by another race as part of the fleet. He didn't trust its manufacturing. When I argued with him, he informed me that arguing, instead of going along with him, was why we pay the tariffs we do for the goods we receive from Tretra. The bastard threatened me with more tariffs, too! He threatened Joth!" President Benter said, clearly angry. "Politics!"

"Look, Harmon, can I call you Harmon? I want to help you out. Frost! I want the ship. But Tretra has us between a rock and a sand pit, and that's just the way it is. The way it has always been. The next thing you know, they'll try to make us collect beings' weapons," he said, shaking his head.

"I even tried to get him to make an exception and have them register it. He told me he would allow the registration office to register it but only if it had a title. He then gave me the price quote to build a medium battlecruiser. He said that was what he would instruct the Tretra Title Commissioner, one of his cronies, to use in assessing the value of the ship. The title fee would cost millions. He doesn't plan on helping at all," the president said.

Harmon knew all new ships built in-system would have to go through Tretra's Spacecraft Title Office before receiving a registration. It was so Tretra could receive the bulk of the fees for titles and registrations within the entire system. It was robbery.

Harmon had an idea. New ships? The battlecruiser wasn't new. The more he thought about it, the more he realized it might actually work. He could get a title.

"Sir, could I ask for a favor?" Harmon asked.

"Absolutely, though I'm not doing very well in that department for you today," the president said.

"Can I borrow your computer?" Harmon asked, nodding toward the president's desk.

"What do you have in mind?" President Benter asked as he stood up and motioned Harmon over.

President Benter watched in silence as Harmon pulled up the title offices on Joth, located in the capitol. He started smiling to himself as he watched Harmon apply for a title and wait a moment for it to process; after it went through, he watched as Harmon applied for registration in the Tretrayon System. After a moment, it came through, and he then watched as Harmon applied for a galaxy registration through the local gate with the Bith. It took a little longer, but it came through. He started laughing and didn't even care that the planet government was paying for the message through the gate.

"I can't believe you just did that," he said, wiping the tear from his eye from laughing so hard.

"Nothing to it, sir," said Harmon. "Sitting here, I realized that I could use the local Vehicle Title Office to get a title. I remember looking at it to see about getting a hovercraft that Rinto owns registered. We had been using it off the yard, and I didn't want to have to pay a fine if I got caught. The site asks a few questions: Does the vehicle roll or fly? Does the vehicle fly more than one foot off the ground? Does the vehicle have a current title? If NO, see age of vehicle. If age of vehicle is over fifty years, see salvage title.

The president started laughing again. "And it only cost you 100 credits because it was over fifty years old. Stop...stop, I can't breathe," he said. He was laughing so hard he was holding his side.

"Hey sir, it's not my fault the title application system didn't specifically say it had to be a planet-based vehicle. I didn't write the regulations. I just found the loophole," Harmon said.

"I know, I know. But did you have to name it *Salvage Title* when you registered it?" The president could barely get the last of his words out, he was laughing so hard.

"Yeah, that was funny, wasn't it?" Harmon asked, then started laughing, too.

* * * * *

Chapter Fifteen

"You got a title?" Clip asked again. He still didn't believe it.

Harmon tossed him his slate. "Check it out. I even got it registered with the galaxy," Harmon said, smiling.

"*Salvage Title?* You named it, *Salvage Title?*" Clip asked, reading the slate.

"That iss hilariouss," Zerith said.

Zerith looked at Clip. Clip looked at Zerith. They both looked at Harmon, and they all burst out laughing. Rinto just looked at all of them, smiled, and shook his head.

"Boys, one day there's not going to be a loophole," he said. "You might want to head out before they realize what you did and try to impound that ship."

"Good idea, we should leave right away," Harmon said, standing up.

"Not until I go sshopping, there iss no more fruit in the galley of the *Hauler*," said Zerith as he sprinted out of Rinto's office.

* * *

They were still using the *Hauler* as the living space in the bay of the battlecruiser; it was easier since they planned to sell it. There was no sense getting used to the larger cabins. Besides, it was a little unnerving with just the seven of them in the huge craft.

That evening, Jayneen broke orbit and laid in a course for the gate. It didn't take long before they were hailed on the comm—the fleet had been keeping a sensor on the battlecruiser. They were registered within the system now, so they were no longer unidentified.

"*Salvage Title*, this is TDF *Trevarta*," a voice came over the comm.

"*Trevarta...Salvage Title*," answered Harmon with a grin as he looked at the commander of the large missile carrier on the screen.

"Why have you left orbit? State your intentions," the stern-looking captain said.

"Exiting the system to meet a potential buyer for the *Salvage Title*," Harmon said.

"Wait one," Captain Loid said. The screen went blank.

"Let me know how it goess," Zerith said. He was headed back to the engine room to check on things. He would probably stop at the *Hauler* for a snack.

Harmon wondered what the conversations were like within the fleet. He knew whatever was being discussed; it probably went all the way up to the system level. He knew they couldn't really stop the battlecruiser unless they fired on it or boarded it. Neither was a likely scenario no matter who he had angered.

"*Salvage Title*...TDF *Trevarta*," a voice said. Jayneen put it on screen.

"*Trevarta...Salvage Title*," Harmon said looking at an ensign. He guessed that whatever he was going to be told, the captain didn't want to be the one to relay it.

"Be advised that the *Salvage Title* is not welcome in this system. Should it return it will be impounded as a threat to the safety of its citizens. Acknowledge...over," said the ensign, looking above his shoulder and not directly at him.

Harmon waited a full thirty seconds before answering. "Roger. *Salvage Title*, out."

"Well, that's that. You want me to hack their supply system and short the toilet paper order on that ship the next time they receive supplies? Because I can, you know," Clip said.

"No," Harmon said. "It's not anyone on that ship's fault. I blame it on the president of the system. It's ridiculous…trying to control honest capitalism. That's what it is."

"Where would you like me to take the ship?" Jayneen asked over the overhead speakers.

"We're going to the Nilta System," Harmon said. "I put an ad out and the buyer there looks the most promising. She agreed to the price: 100 million credits. I can't even picture that kind of money."

"Would you like me to show it to you on the screen?" the AI asked.

"Just a figure of speech, Jayneen," said Harmon.

"What are we going to do with it all?" Clip asked, turning toward Harmon.

"Pay the crew, buy a bigger salvage ship, hire some more folks and go make some more credits, I guess. I never thought we would make this kind of credit…ever," Harmon said.

It was a ridiculous amount. A new ship of this size would have cost a lot more to build, but Harmon couldn't ask that price. They were headed to a small system two days' gate time away. Harmon hadn't heard of it before his advertisement was answered by a Krift, an insectoid race. They looked like seven-foot-tall ants. Apparently the being he had communicated with was in charge of system defense there and wished to purchase the ship.

"I did a little research; this place doesn't have the best reputation. It doesn't even have anyone assigned to guard the gate," Clip said.

"I agree. There are several supply companies who have publicly announced they will no longer trade in that system," the AI added.

"That's why I have a plan," Harmon said.

Harmon was going to fly the Zax out of the *Hauler's* bay...out of the battlecruiser's bay. He would fly it into the space port that was only five hours from the gate. The deal would be conducted there. Once the transaction was complete, Harmon would fly back and land in the *Hauler* and then collect Clip, Zerith, and the crew from the battlecruiser. They would leave the bay open so the new owners could occupy their craft. It was too easy. What could go wrong?

* * *

In the Nilta System, on board the Q-ship *Awaken,* Tachell rubbed her top two legs together. She looked over with her multifaceted eyes at her second in command, a young female Krift, while her antennae spread apart repeatedly. It was a sign of impatience among her race. Twill was standing over the weapons drone as he selected several missiles and relayed the information to the drones in the forward compartment. The missile tubes had been added to the converted freighter and had to be manually loaded. It was best to be ready.

If Tachell had to use missiles on the ship, she wanted to be sure that they would not cause too much damage. The missiles the drone selected would provide a large magnetic pulse when they struck the target, causing systems to temporarily go offline. With well-placed shots, her soldiers could board the powerless battlecruiser and take it quickly.

Her intention was to pull away from the space dock when the fool that she was meeting was close. If she waited until the battlecruiser was far enough from the gate, she could chase it down. She would destroy his transport ship and then take the battlecruiser. She had no intention of paying for it.

Tachell paid for nothing. Especially in this system. It was hers. The system paid her. She collected protection fees from the space port, any merchant ships that entered the system, and the planet itself. The docile beings were only too happy to pay after she threatened to drop a few meteors on their heads.

The system had hardly any space traffic before she and her small swarm descended on it, and her tactics hadn't harmed its trade that much. The Nilt's only export of note was the thick liquid sweetener used in cooking by several systems. They farmed it from huge flowering trees on the surface of Nilta, the fourth planet from the slightly orange-tinted star. It was actually a poor planet as far as systems within the galaxy went, but she still demanded payment.

There was another planet in the system with an atmosphere, but it was uninhabited. A world of sand and rock. She never bothered to learn its name.

The Nilts had built a small space port to service the haulers they used to ship the sweetener. It was her base of operations now. Its manager had been kicked out of her office and quarters. She had four ships docked there: her Q-ship, two small freighters that were Q-ships, and a small local hauler. The hauler had been converted to a modified dropship that would carry her soldiers to the battlecruiser to board it.

She still could not believe her luck in convincing the human she was willing to purchase the ship. She clacked her mandibles quietly together as she thought of descending upon the next system with a warship at her control. She could create an empire. The fool had even let her know it was coming with a skeleton crew when she had inquired about the number of beings needed to operate it. This was too easy. What could go wrong?

* * * * *

Chapter Sixteen

Salvage Title exited the gate into a system with just six planets orbiting its light orange sun. It was five hours from the gate to the space port where Harmon was going to meet Tachell. Jayneen turned the ship and slowed it down as it came into the system. They had entered the gate at a slow rate of speed so it wouldn't take too much time to slow and stop the battlecruiser well away from the space port.

Harmon eased the Zax out of the *Hauler* into the bay. Once the deal was done, Clip was going to disconnect the AI from the battlecruiser and wait for Harmon to come back and land the Zax. She definitely wasn't going with the ship.

He eased the Zax out of the battlecruiser's bay and turned it toward the port. He kicked in the thrust and shot away, feeling little of the G-forces. The suit he had purchased to help reduce the effects of high-G was working fine. It was credits well spent.

"Be careful, man; I still don't like this whole arrangement," said Clip over the comms. "It seems to me this Krift could have met us in a neutral system. Like, maybe a system where she is not in charge of its defense. Everything I've read about this system has not been good. The only thing the net has that's good to say about this place is that the main export is pretty good in a glass of tea, for what that's worth."

"I'll be fine," Harmon answered back.

Harmon was ten minutes from the port when he noticed a large ship back away from it and turn toward him on his sensor. Three other ships pulled away shortly after, leaving no ships docked to the port at all. Something funny was going on. He eased off the thrusters and called back to the battlecruiser.

"Hey Clip, do you see this?" Harmon asked.

"We see it. It looks like a welcoming party. What do you want to do? We're two hours from the port and three hours from the gate. We are also at a dead stop, but it wouldn't take too long to pick up some speed," Clip said

"I'm turning back now. Frost!" Harmon said, turning the fighter back toward the battlecruiser.

"Do not make me destroy you," a translated voice said over the comm. "Turn around and dock at the port. I will have that ship. You cannot escape through the gate in time; I will fire upon the battle-cruiser. You yourself told me there is a skeleton crew. You cannot fight the ship."

Harmon kicked in the thrusters in an attempt to get away. The big ship was eight minutes behind him and picking up speed. He glanced at his sensor and saw two missiles separate from the ship and streak toward him. The missiles would catch him. They were not piloted, and G-forces were irrelevant. They were gaining.

"*They just fired missiles!*" Clip screamed over the comm.

"I know, I see them. Not so loud, you almost burst my eardrums. I hear you just fine," said Harmon.

Harmon was thinking. He had never expected to be fired on. He checked his gauges. There was plenty of fuel and he had the lasers. Would he be able to hit a missile with the weapons on the fighter?

He banked hard and came back around, and his computer lined up his reticle on a missile and started firing. His rate of fire was double what it had been when new; Zerith had beefed it up. He hit the missile and it went twisting off to his starboard side.

The computer lined up his sights on the second missile; it was going to be close. He fired off a shot and banked hard around. He needed some distance between him and that ship. He lined up his heading for the battlecruiser, cut the thrusters, and flipped the fighter around. He was still headed for the *Salvage Title,* but now he was facing the missile and the incoming ship. He lined up the reticle using his small maneuvering thrusters and squeezed the trigger. The fourth blast hit the missile, and it exploded with a blinding flash at the outer edge of the missile's effective kill radius. His engines went out, his panel started flickering, and then everything went offline.

Harmon tried resetting the systems one by one, but they would not come up. He unplugged from the ship's environmental system. It was going to get really cold really fast. His suit had an emergency air supply good for eight hours…if the heater in his suit didn't run the battery down first. And if the next missile didn't destroy the craft.

He tried resetting the comms again, but they still didn't work. The missile that had hit him also had a magnetic pulse that had killed his equipment; he was amazed it hadn't affected his suit. The Q-ship was coming, though, and there was no way for him to avoid it. Even with the distance he had put between them, it would be there within the hour. He was drifting at a pretty good speed toward the battlecruiser, but that Q-ship was under power and accelerating. He wasn't going to make it.

* * *

Clip was watching the sensor screens and saw the Q-ship gaining on the Zax. Jayneen had turned the big ship and was headed toward Harmon. She told Clip that if they got close enough, she could engage a tractor beam and draw the fighter in. It was a system designed to pull fighters, small craft, and rescue pods into the bay of the battlecruiser. It wouldn't stop a ship under power, but it could reach out and hold a small craft that was drifting.

"*They have launched*," Vera said in muffled voice over the comms.

"Vera? Who launched...launched what?" Clip said, as he noticed two small ships exit the bay of the ancient battlecruiser.

"We are going to get Harmon," Zerith said. "I am in the mech. Hank and Sstan are wearing two of the light battle armor ssuitss and piloting the fighterss. I am locked to the landing gear of Hank'ss fighter. It is very excciting."

"They will reach Harmon before the Q-ship reaches him at the rate they are traveling," Jayneen said. "Though, the calculations change. The fighters are not flying in a straight path toward the Zax."

"They're all crazy," Clip said, sitting back. "This is a ship of fools."

* * *

A flash caught Harmon's attention. He couldn't believe what he was seeing. One of the sleek alien fighters from the *Salvage Title* was lining up above and in front of his fighter as it drifted backward, and it had the mech locked to its landing strut. He hoped the fighter didn't get too close and smash the mech through his cockpit.

He wondered who was in the war machine. *It had to be Zerith…did that mean Clip was flying the fighter?* He didn't know who else it could be. Then he saw the other fighter loop around and fire missiles at the Q-ship. *Frost! That meant the brothers were flying the fighters. This was definitely not good. Whoever thought up this plan was not sane.*

* * *

"I can't believe Zerith let them get into the cockpits of those fighters. Is he insane?" Clip asked Jayneen again. He continued to try to contact Harmon and watched the sensors.

Hank disengaged the magnets on the struts and pulled away from the Zax. He was going to join his brother and attack the big ship. Flying a fighter was great fun! He had never flown anything other than a small shuttle before back in his home system. He reached up and pushed the helmet back up so he could see. The alien battle suit was just a little large, but the helmet almost fit his head since it was shaped similar to his. He had tied the bottom two sleeves into a knot at his waist and the suit was rolled up and tied off above his feet. It leaked a little, but he could breathe, so that was good.

"You. This is me, over," Hank said, using the comms in his helmet.

"Roger, you. This is me," Stan answered.

He banked around and fired two missiles at the ship lined up in his reticle. It was not the big ship, it was one slightly behind and to the side. That was okay. He had more missiles. He applied more thrust and grinned as the G-forces pushed him down.

"Roger, you. I am going after the small ones. You fight the big one. This is me. Out," Hank said.

"Roger that, you. This is me. Out," Stan answered.

Zerith tapped the thrusters in the mech and flew down to the Zax. The thrusters were powerful enough to fly the suit in gravity with all of its weight. In space it was weightless, so there was plenty of thrust for what he wanted to do. He flew past the cockpit and grabbed the engine housing. He turned himself around, locked the claws into the fighter, hit the thrusters full output, pushed one leg out, and turned its nose toward the battlecruiser. It was very exciting.

* * *

S tan leaned his head back so he could see better and watched as his missiles hit the shield in front of the ship. He could see it shimmer a light blue color when they struck. He shrugged inside his oversized suit and fired the remaining six missiles at the Q-ship and squeezed the trigger on the lasers. Maybe he could overload the shield. He looked over to his port side and saw his brother heading around the ship. He looked back and saw two missiles leave the Q-ship right before four of his missiles exploded against the ship. There was a bright flash that caused his goggles to darken. They cleared after a moment; the ship was hit and venting atmosphere in a number of places!

He flew back and forth, squeezing the trigger, as internal explosions tore the big ship apart. Occasionally he could feel the shudder as his fighter was hit by laser fire from the ship, but his shields held.

This was great. He would ask Harmon if he could fly it again some-time. He was not even wobbling anymore. Flying a fighter wasn't so hard once you got used to how fast they went. The shuttle back home could not do this.

Hank watched the two missiles hit the small ship and tear a hole in its side. He could see atmosphere spraying from the ship. Its engines were still firing, so he lined up his reticle on them and launched another missile. He looked at his sensor for another ship. Two were turning away from him. He followed. This was loads of fun.

Hank launched two missiles at the smallest ship. His fighter lurched as some warning lights came on in the display. He couldn't read them, but the little image of his ship on a screen showed that his shield was down. He liked the little screen; he could fire missiles just by touching their symbol twice. The laser blasts he had been taking from all three ships had overloaded the shield. He decided he shouldn't fly in a straight path. He began weaving and rolling the fighter. He fired his last three missiles at the other ship and turned away. He was down to half engine output. That was okay. He could fix that. Maybe...once he took it apart to see how it worked.

* * *

Tachell watched as the two missiles left her ship toward the fleeing craft. They would stop it and continue past to capture the battlecruiser. One of the missiles flew off away from the craft. She leaned forward and could now tell it was a fighter. The second missile exploded, but the fighter was within range of its pulse. Its engine shut down.

"It is powerless, my queen," said the drone at the tactical console.

She was watching the screen and waving her antennae impatiently as they closed in on the ship. She leapt to her legs when she saw two more fighters leave the battlecruiser on the sensor screen. How could they launch fighters? They were a skeleton crew.

"They have launched more fighters," her second said. "These are different; I have no idea of their capabilities. There is no information on the net, and their readings are strange. I am working on it, My Queen," she added.

They were gaining on the drifting fighter. She saw the battlecruiser was coming to them instead of fleeing. She was sure the fighters could be dealt with. The shields should be able to withstand a fighter's laser fire. She would have that ship.

"Full power to forward shields!" Tachell screamed as she watched two missiles appear from one fighter. "Fire all lasers!" The other fighter had merged with the powerless fighter. Seconds later, she saw it peel away and turn toward them. The Q-ship rocked, causing her to spread her wings slightly for balance.

"Forward shields down to fifty percent, My Queen," called out her second.

The *Awaken*, a converted merchant ship, had shields, but they were not military grade. Too many of those missiles and it would fail. She watched in horror as the same fighter launched six missiles at once. She sat back down.

"Fire the last two missiles," she ordered, "and tell the others to flee." She knew the shield would fail. She had been lied to. They had many crew members. *How dare that human lie,* was her last thought.

* * * * *

Chapter Seventeen

Harmon watched the second fighter land in the bay. It bounced and skidded a few feet to a stop right behind the first fighter, throwing sparks as its landing strut scraped the bay floor. Neither craft was anywhere near where it was supposed to sit in line with the others. He still couldn't believe that someone had actually thought it was a good idea to let them pilot fighters.

He felt the Zax shake slightly as his ship was pulled in toward an open area of the bay. Once inside, it dropped with a clang, and he felt the fighter shake again as the mech slid off the back. The doors to the bay were closing, and he looked over to see who was at the control panel. Vera and Kyla stood by the panel, both wearing oversized battle armor. The sleeves were too long, the legs were bunched up, and Kyla was holding her helmet back so she could peer through the visor. *What the frost is going on around here? I leave for a few hours, and they go insane.*

When the environmental system cleared the bay, Harmon manually opened the cockpit of the Zax. He stood in the seat and looked around the bay. Zerith was climbing out of the mech. Both brothers were standing by the smoking fighter, holding a helmet in one hand and waving their other hand around, mimicking the flight of a fighter. They were talking rapidly in growls, hisses, and whistles. He pulled his earpiece out. It wasn't working; the translation wasn't

145

coming through. He had a pretty good idea what they were talking about, though.

Vera's helmet was lying on the floor of the bay as she struggled to help Kyla get her helmet off. She turned it slightly, and it came loose; then they both ambled over to their mates. Their conversation got louder. Harmon sat on the edge of the cockpit and shook his head. All four of them looked ridiculous with their suits bunched up like accordions. *Insane.*

* * *

"I swear I didn't have anything to do with it," Clip said. "Tell him, Jayneen. We're innocent."

"That is correct. I was not monitoring the bay or the *Hauler*. I am not insane," Jayneen said.

Everyone was on the bridge of the battlecruiser. Jayneen had slowed the ship to almost a complete stop as they contemplated their next decision.

"I just want to know who came up with the crazy idea to let Hank and Stan pilot fighters. Especially since we had no idea of their true capabilities, exactly how to fly them, and how to use the weapons. You brought the mech out to act as an engine. Really, Zerith?" Harmon asked.

"It wass not my idea," Zerith said around a mouthful of berries.

"If it wasn't made on the bridge and you didn't do it, whose idea was it?" Harmon asked, confused.

Three Leethog and the Prithmar looked at Kyla, who tilted her head to the side and smiled, showing all her teeth. She had reapplied lipstick.

Kyla was the smallest and the quietest crew member. She spoke to the other Leethog but rarely spoke to Harmon and Clip. It didn't make any sense.

"Kyla?" Harmon implored. He had an earpiece and a spare comm, so he could now understand them.

"Well," Kyla said. "You were being attacked. Clip said so over the comms. We could not let them kill you. Pirates are very bad. Everyone knows this. The fastest way to get to you was in one of the fighters. They are very fast. Clip said the Zax was in one piece but had no power. I thought someone should go get you. I told Hank-tilmotal to go."

"I was giving a running commentary," admitted Clip.

"If Hanktilmotal was going to fly a fighter, I was going to fly a fighter. He cannot have all the fun," Stan stated. The other three Leethog nodded their heads in agreement.

"And the mech?" Harmon asked, looking at Zerith.

"I couldn't let them capture you, either," Zerith said. "I knew that the mech could be your engine. I made the thrussterss in it. It is a fine dessign." All the Leethog nodded in agreement.

Harmon shook his head, smiling. He couldn't really be angry. It was a stunt he might have pulled…and it *had* saved his life.

"What's the deal with the battle suits, then? What was that all about?" Harmon asked.

"Well, they needed to breathe in the fighters. We do not know what the ratio of oxygen is in the cockpit. They had already put comms in all of the suits while we were in orbit around Joth. Sometimes the men take things apart and make them better," Kyla said, like she was revealing a huge secret. "The suits had comms and the oxygen ratio had been set. And they needed some protection. What if they got shot? The suits we have do not provide any protection. And they fit us. Almost," Kyla said, holding up an arm with a rolled sleeve. She had taken her gloves off.

"But flying the fighters...I looked at the controls. It takes four hands. How did you manage that?" Harmon asked, looking back at the wannabe fighter pilots.

They looked down at their feet. Harmon looked down, too. Below the rolled-up pant legs on Hank and Stan, their feet were bare. It was the first time he had seen their feet without work boots on. Each foot had three fingers and an opposable thumb.

Harmon thought about the fighter's cockpit. The seat was designed in a reclining position. The more he thought about it, he realized that there weren't any foot pedals. Everything was designed to be operated by that race's four hands. He was beginning to rethink selling the battlecruiser.

Harmon had to smile as the Leethog wiggled their toes at him. "Thanks, everybody; I mean that," he said.

While Harmon was talking with the Leethog, Clip had been looking at the sensor screen. He couldn't see any signs of power from any of the four ships. They were all drifting, and if they wanted to make some credits off the salvage of those ships, they needed to stop them.

"Jayneen, can the tractor beams lock onto those ships if we get near?" he asked.

"Yes, I believe so. If they do not have their thrusters operating, that is," Jayneen said.

"Let's run them down, then," Harmon said.

The crew left the bridge, talking among themselves. Zerith followed shortly after to check on things in the engine room. It was quiet for a minute.

Clip looked at Harmon and said, "The mech was hooked to the fighter." He was grinning.

"I don't think even I would have done that," Harmon said. And he meant it.

* * * * *

Chapter Eighteen

They managed to stop the four damaged ships, and it took them two days to move them to the same area. They put them in a high orbit around the last planet in the system, a small, frozen planet.

During the process, they pulled twenty-two survivors from the wrecks. An additional twelve were saved from escape pods. Once they were brought onboard by Harmon in the mech, they were marched by Hank and Stan to a compartment with one door and were locked in. They gave no sign of resistance; it was almost as if they had no purpose and were lost.

Hank and Stan piled their weapons in the weapons vault. They had taken quite a few pistols and several rifles from the Krift. Zerith and the brothers removed several laser turrets from the smallest ship. He figured they might be something he could mount on the *Hauler*.

They took their prisoners to the space port. When they docked and entered the port, a Nilt was waiting for them. She was four feet long, almost round, and hovering about five feet off the deck. Harmon could hear her wings buzzing but couldn't see them as more than a blur. Behind her were a dozen smaller yellow and black Nilt, also hovering.

"I am Lilith, queen of this port. Do you wish for us to pay for protection?" the Nilt asked through the translator.

"Pay? No. We will do well salvaging their ships," Harmon said. "We have some prisoners for you. I'm sure your system can try them for piracy and deal with them."

"We can do this. They will be put to work on the farms. There are several queens that would gladly take them and work them until they die," she said.

"Until they die? It beats being executed, I guess," Clip said.

"They get what they desserve," Zerith stated.

"I am prepared to purchase the ships from you. My workers can salvage them. We are willing to pay now for the salvage rights. Consider it our thanks," the Nilt said.

It was hard to pass up. Getting paid without having to spend the time salvaging the ships was a sweet deal. Harmon was really thinking about not selling the battlecruiser now. Maybe they should try and figure out how to hire a crew. They could go back to visit Joth on the *Hauler* and keep a crew on *Salvage Title* in a nearby system.

They spent a day at the port finalizing the deal for the ships and making sure the credits hit their accounts, which were starting to look impressive. The crew members looked at their personal accounts and were at a loss for words. The ships could eventually be repaired. It would cost a lot, but it was far cheaper than purchasing new ships. The Nilt had a small shipyard orbiting their planet and could do it. They paid eight million credits.

"Where should we go? We can't go home, that's for sure," Clip said as they were headed toward the gate.

"Anywhere iss fine with me," Zerith said. He was happy he had scored two jars of the sweetener.

"I don't know," Harmon said. "Maybe we should hire a crew and hunt pirates. A lot of systems will pay good credit to anyone that rids their system of them. You can find inquiries right on the net."

"Where would we get a crew?" Clip asked. "You want a ship full of Leethog taking things apart and putting them back together? I heard all the male Leethog are that way. Too curious for their own good. Why do you think that when Kyla gave Hank his orders, he jumped? I think the females in that race are the level-headed ones."

"Harmon, Clip, Zerith," Jayneen interrupted. "I think you should watch the news videos. The entire first fleet of the Tretrayon Defense Fleet is no more." The AI put the galactic news feed on the main screen.

There was a story from the Leatara system. Leatara was a human world that had an ongoing dispute with the Squilla over mining rights, a recurring thing with them. The Squilla would swoop in when there were new discoveries and claim they had been there first. Lately, no one had prospected near their system.

It seemed the rumors Evelyn had told him were true. Half of the Tretrayon Fleet had gone to the Leatara system, hired as a show of force. The twenty-eight ships had more than doubled the number of ships defending the system.

A total of one hundred Squilla warships had come through the gate. They had lost fifty of them but had destroyed the entire defense force. There would be no rescue for the survivors of the fleet, either, as the Squilla traditionally let rescue pods float. History had shown they didn't answer distress calls.

Only one ship, the heavy battlecruiser TDF *Carthon,* had managed to escape through the gate. Reports were that it was running on one fusion plant and leaking atmosphere. That was the ship Evelyn was attached to—it held an entire company of Marines.

Harmon knew that even if Evelyn survived that battle, she might not survive the next. The Squilla would finish destroying that planet and would claim it as their own. Then, when the Squilla were done with Leatara, they would seek revenge against the system that had helped stand against them.

And, in that part of the galaxy, there would be no rescue coming. Other races would not come to Tretra's aid. Earth was too far removed to worry about it. There was no "human alliance." Tretra had sent the fleet to Leatara for credits and no other reason. The Tretrayon System was on its own, and the Squilla would come. They knew the system was vulnerable.

"Jayneen. Lay in the coordinates for the Leethog System," Harmon said.

"Leethog? You mean..." Clip asked, his eyes wide.

"Yep, we're about to go get us a crew...God help us," Harmon said. "Call the crew to the bridge, please, Zerith."

* * * * *

Chapter Nineteen

Many races traded with the Leethog and came to the system to hire crew members, and *Salvage Title* came through the gate into a system teeming with traffic. Harmon had explained to the crew what happened to the Tretrayon's fleet and that he intended to get a full crew and see what the battle-cruiser was capable of. Whoever he hired would have to learn quickly, because he intended to take the ship back to Joth and help defend the system. When he asked them if they would like to stay onboard or be taken home, they didn't hesitate—their answer was to stay.

"Are you sure? Why do you want to stay? It is going to be dangerous. None of us may survive," Harmon said, moved that they would not consider leaving.

Kyla tilted her head, pushed her goggles up on her forehead, and said, "We are associates."

"What? I don't understand," Harmon said. He looked at Clip and Zerith, and they both shrugged.

"Associates. Tomeral and Associates. We are associates. We receive a percentage of profit. We do not receive a salary. Whoever you hire will be paid a salary. Correct?" she asked.

"Well, yes, I guess they will," Harmon said, starting to understand.

"They will be employees, not associates," Vera explained, as if it made all the sense in the galaxy.

Three heads were bobbing. Clip and Zerith smiled and bobbed their heads in imitation. Harmon just shook his and smiled back. If nothing else, he had loyal friends.

"Well, you just got a raise in percentage," Harmon said. He looked over at his friends.

"Five perccent each," Zerith said.

Harmon thought it was fair but was surprised. Zerith was kind of tight with his credits. Clip nodded. There were teeth everywhere on four nodding heads.

"We are going to your home world, anyway," Harmon said. "We need a crew, and your people seem to specialize in hiring onto ships and living away from your system."

"We do," Hank said. "It can be very boring on our world. Everything has already been taken apart and fixed. Idle hands can get one into trouble. You will have no problem finding Leethog to do the job."

"And," Kyla added, right before they left the bridge, "they better do their job well or they will answer to me." At this, Hank and Stan stopped smiling and nodded their heads slowly. She was serious.

There was a large spaceport near the planet Leethog. Harmon called ahead to reserve a berth. It had forty docking arms, and twenty-eight were already occupied. The ships there ranged from small personal craft to huge vacation liners. Several merchant ships too big to dock waited nearby. Cargo shuttles could be seen coming and going, either loading or offloading goods. There was definitely more activity here than their home system ever saw.

"*Salvage Title*. Defense Platform 10," a translated voice came over the comm.

Jayneen put it on the screen for Harmon to answer. Clip looked up from his slate where he had been writing a program. Harmon had no idea what it was.

"Defense Platform 10. *Salvage Title,*" Harmon answered, looking at a Leethog in a uniform.

"Please state your destination and intentions," he said.

"This is a privately-owned ship. We intend to dock at the spaceport and post a help wanted advertisement in the system. We are looking to hire a full crew," Harmon said.

"Our sensors indicate you are a warship, are you not?" the Leethog asked.

"That is correct," Harmon said, not sure where this was going.

The Leethog on-screen muted the call, and Harmon could see him turn and look away from his screen. His hands were moving everywhere as he spoke. His head started bobbing, and there was that grin. Clip looked over and raised an eyebrow.

"*Salvage Title,* would you be interested in an experienced weapons crew of ten?" he asked.

"Absolutely. We will be docked at berth thirty-six until we have filled all positions," Harmon said.

"This may be easier than we thought," Clip said.

"There will be Leethog throughout my ship...our ship. You know what I mean. I will be distressed until they put back together everything that they take apart. Please tell me that you have a good hunch, Harmon," the AI said.

"Don't sweat it, Jayneen. What could go wrong?" Harmon responded.

"I do not sweat, and I have heard that before," the AI answered.

Clip posted an advertisement on the local system's help wanted board. Harmon made sure the ad said it would be a dangerous job. They didn't want to mislead anyone. The *Salvage Title* was a warship, and they *would* see action.

They received over three hundred replies within the first two hours. Zerith suggested that Jayneen go through the applications and narrow it down to people with actual experience in the positions they needed to fill as she knew the ship and what they were looking for.

The entire crew from Defense Platform 10 was hired, as well as crews from two other platforms. Six pilots from one of the destroyers in the Leethog's fleet applied. Harmon realized a lot of members of the local fleet were applying. He had Jayneen put in a call to the commander of the fleet. She had no problem securing a link to the headquarters comm.

"Ma'am, I am Harmon Tomeral. We may have a situation here, and I would like to clarify some things before I upset you and the system government," Harmon said.

Jayneen had placed the call and put it on-screen. An admiral in full uniform was looking at him. She was an older Leethog with whiter fur on her face than her crewmembers.

"Lieutenant Tomeral, I recognize you. I was very interested in your system's fleet Marine competition. I feel we could use something like that here in our system. Let me offer you a belated congratulations," Fleet Admiral Lucytileerlot said.

"Thank you, ma'am," Harmon said, a little surprised word had spread this far.

"I understand some of my fleet may be looking to jump ship," she said.

Harmon winced. "It was never my intention to cause that, ma'am," he said.

"I have given permission for a leave of absence to any that wishes to obtain combat experience. It is not something that can be obtained in our system. It is their choice," she said.

"Ma'am, I can't guarantee that any will make it back home," Harmon said.

"That is the nature of our profession, Lieutenant. I wish you good luck," she said as she signed off.

Within three days, the *Salvage Title* had a full crew of experienced members. Harmon had hired one hundred and fifty Leethog. The eight of them, including Jayneen, had discussed the fact that extra personnel could come in handy if there were injuries or emergency repairs that needed to be made. It was a somber discussion.

Harmon figured they had about ten more days to shake out the ancient battlecruiser and see what it was capable of. For the first three days, he spent the time trying to learn who was working in the critical positions as the new crew turned the ship upside down, learning what its systems were capable of. Weapons, tactical, flight operations, engine rooms, and medical. There were many more positions on the ship, and Harmon wondered if he had bitten off more than he could chew.

Normally the commander of a ship the size of *Salvage Title* would have decades of experience. They would have started as an ensign, assigned a duty position on a ship. They would have learned many different positions as they advanced in experience and rank. Their first command would be a small ship, a cutter or a corvette with a small crew.

On the third day, Kyla came to the bridge. She was wearing a uniform like the rest of the crew members. Harmon wondered where she got it. He did a double take. There was no patch on the shoulder, but she had a rank on her collar.

"Hi, Kyla," Harmon said. "Um, what are you wearing?"

"I work for Senior Chief Warrant Officer Farnog. I am a technician. It is my power plant. Every being assigned to work there works for me. This is the flagship of Tomeral and Associates and I am a chief warrant officer. I have studied fleet rank. You are a captain," Kyla said.

"Whoa, slow down. Captain? Not hardly," Harmon said.

"I have been listening to the Leethog speaking to each other. They refer to you as the captain, Clip as the commander, and Zerith as the senior chief warrant officer," Jayneen said.

"This has gone too far," Harmon said.

"No, I think Kyla is right. If you're going to lead this crew into a battle, you have to have the rank. I've never been in any type of military, and even I know that," Clip said.

"But captain?" Harmon asked.

"I have brought these uniforms for you," Kyla said, putting down the bundle she had been holding. "They are your sizes," she added.

"Thanks, I guess," Harmon said.

"Oh, and Lieutenant Commander Jayneen, could you change the translations on all systems from Earth Common to Leethog? I think things will go much smoother," Kyla asked, looking up at the console.

"Yes, I can do that," the AI answered.

"Thank you," said the chief warrant officer. She left the bridge.

"Why didn't we think of that?" Clip asked.

"She called me lieutenant commander," the AI said.

"Well…Lieutenant Commander Seven-Eleven-Two-whatever else it is, don't change my station to Leethog. Clip may be smart enough to learn it, but I don't know how to read whistles, growls, and hisses," Harmon said. He threw a uniform to Clip and went to find Zerith.

Later, as he stepped out of the lift, he noticed there was a different feel to the battlecruiser. It was as if the old girl had gained a life of its own. There were the sounds of fighters leaving the ship and coming in for landings, the slight vibrations as turrets turned as one to lock in on imagined targets, and the sound of the Leethog talking in their rapid language.

It was discovered that the ship had full missile racks including enough in reserve to reload all their racks three times. Harmon figured that it was enough for three battles, but he hoped they would not find out. Once they were out of missiles, there wouldn't be any more, and the entire missile system would have to be replaced to accommodate missiles that he could purchase.

He was relieved to find out the missiles onboard had powerful warheads. Jayneen assured him the records showed they were very destructive, but *not* radioactive. The last thing they needed was to use some kind of ancient nuclear weapon. One hint of that, and the Bith would shut down the gate in the offender's system permanently. This had happened to two systems he knew of. He had learned about them in Galactic Military History 101.

The ship had hundreds of small lasers mounted on its hull. They were networked together in groups as close anti-missile defense. They were next to last resort, ahead of the shields.

There were eighty small sliding hatches on the ship. Beneath the hatches were racks of four small missiles. They were smaller than the missiles the fighters carried, only the size of Harmon's forearm. They served the same anti-missile purpose the lasers did, but they would stop missiles farther out. In the head of each missile was a shaped charge with a handful of steel balls. A missile moving at incredible speed would be devastated if it met a single ball.

They were "fire and forget" weapons. The rockets quickly burned through their fuel; however, they reached an incredible speed in that time.

All of this was tied into the tactical officer's position and the weapons console on the bridge. It was also connected to the defensive bridge in the center of the ship. Jayneen had explained the purpose of the defensive bridge was close defense. The room and its occupants were not responsible for evasive maneuvers; instead, they monitored the long-range sensors and computers that determined the best firing solutions to destroy incoming missiles before they reached the shields. Four consoles and a slightly raised command center filled the compartment. Now that Harmon had crew members who could pilot the ship, he decided that Clip should handle the defensive bridge with Jayneen there to aid in calculations and give the ship a better chance of surviving battles. It allowed the crew of the command bridge the freedom to maneuver and fight without worrying about defense as much.

Twelve large pulse cannons were mounted within the ship. They could fire every ten seconds after recharging the energy banks at each site. There were two on the bow and the stern. With four port and starboard, they used a great deal of energy. A portion of it was diverted from each of the four reactors on the ship. It was designed to ensure there would be no power loss to the cannons, even if a reactor failed.

They practiced firing the cannons at asteroids to ensure the targeting was accurate. The pulse could be felt by everyone on board. It wasn't something that interrupted other operations, but there was no doubt when they fired. The energy blast would pound shields until they overloaded and then pound the vessel. The asteroids broke off in chunks. If they worked like Jayneen had described against shields, the Squilla were in for a nasty surprise.

Most fleets relied on missiles as their primary offensive weapons and lasers when the ships came close enough. Lasers would overload shields, but it took time. Blunt force against shields was a different matter, hence the preferred missiles. *Salvage Title* was just a medium battlecruiser, but the pulse cannon, an ancient weapon by an extinct race, was the great equalizer.

Down in the bay, the pilots practiced taking off and landing in the sleek fighters. The bay became an actual flight deck. Hatches were sealed, the artificial gravity was turned off in that section, and the bay was open to space. Everyone working on deck was suited with Leethog-manufactured suits. The new hires had brought their own with them. The boots were magnetized, and a thin cable was tethered to each suit and clipped to rings set in the deck. Harmon was amazed at how the experienced flight deck crew members moved around as if zero gravity was no hindrance, hooked up at all times.

He had been watching from an observation clear-steel window when he decided to suit up and check on the Zax. It was fully repaired and ready to fly. It was too bad he couldn't mount the fighter missiles to his craft like the others. The damaged sleek fighter had been repaired, as well. He watched as Hank and Stan taught the experienced pilots how to fly the ancient fighters. The experienced pilots taught the lieutenants how to fly in formation and properly use the comms; Harmon had heard from Clip about the brothers' first use of it while flying.

As he was leaving the bay area and exiting through the connecting chamber, a room that would cycle the atmosphere so beings could leave the open flight deck, Hank and Stan walked over. They were wearing gloves on all four limbs. *Nice*, thought Harmon. At least their feet wouldn't get cold this time.

"Did you see what we did to your Zax?" Hank asked.

Harmon turned quickly to him. "What did you do?" Harmon asked. "It looked fine."

"We attached a bomb bay," Stan said.

"A what?" Harmon asked.

"A bomb bay. We put the entire case of incendiary grenades in it," Hank said. "You can make one bomb run and drop them all. They will cause a lot of damage. The commander said the mixture is stronger than thermite. I think they may even burn through a hull...maybe."

"Um, thanks," Harmon said.

He couldn't see a situation where he would use them, but it was nice to know they were available. It actually wasn't a bad idea. It would be a surprise to a ship's crew as they were exposed to space with melted hull dripping in.

Zerith, Kyla, and Vera ran their people through drills where they shut down and restarted the fusion plants and engines. Every being in their department was competent, and Kyla only had to tell them once when they erred for corrections to be made. Vera paced back and forth in the engine room, watching the specialists put panels back on after they had looked in and inspected them, learning what they could about the engines they had never seen before.

Emergency repair crews rushed all over the ship, learning their way around without the use of lifts in case of power failure. They also were the team that would fight if boarders needed to be repelled, like Marines in most fleets. They had many extra hands because of the decision to hire extra crew. The Leethog in charge of the repair crew was a really fast talking being named Staff Sergeant Jontilictick. He was the largest Leethog Harmon had seen yet at over five-feet tall and stout. When he barked out a location, his teams scrambled. Harmon liked him; he reminded him of a drill instructor he once had. Big Jon didn't take no lip.

Clip had Jayneen upload the program he wrote. It changed the oscillating pattern of the ship's shields, making them twice as strong as they already were. It had taken him a while to grasp the programming technique used by its creators, but with Jayneen's help, he was able to finish it in time.

They were as ready as they were going to be with five days left, and it was time to head through the gate. He made one last call in the system.

"Ma'am, I want to thank you again. Your fleet members are well-disciplined professionals. Many of them came on board with equipment and gear they thought they would need. I'm sure you had a hand in that, as well," Harmon said.

"You are welcome, though I can neither confirm nor deny that, Captain," the admiral said.

"My system brought this down upon themselves by getting involved against the Squilla. I would hate for it to happen here," Harmon said.

"If the Squilla come here, we will be ready. But they would never consider it. Many races are friends with Leethog. Unlike your system, they would have to battle our neighbors as well as us. It would not bode well for them. And...they are cowards and only attack those that cannot stand against them," the admiral said.

"In my language, we call that a bully, ma'am," Harmon said.

"Indeed. Take care of my niece, Captain Tomeral. Good luck," she said as she signed off.

Niece? Harmon thought. "Captain to Engineering," he said over the comm.

* * * * *

Chapter Twenty

*S*alvage *Title* came through the gate in the Tretrayon System moving just ten percent below the capabilities of its G-force dampener. Harmon had planned to be in orbit around Joth inside of four days of entering the system so the ship was moving fast. He figured it would give him a day or two to deal with the system government and the issues he expected by returning with the ship. He was wrong.

As soon as they emerged, the tactical officer, Lieutenant Adamtilabon, cried out, "Contact! Twenty ships inbound…ahead of us by one day. Three ships within missile range off to starboard, headed away. All ships are confirmed Squilla."

They had come earlier than Harmon had thought, and he hoped they weren't too late. The Squilla must really be angry at Tretra's interference.

"Battle stations, all hands battle stations," Harmon said over the ship's comms.

"All missile launchers online, sir," said Lieutenant Bevtilattley, the weapons officer.

"Sir, I read one medium battlecruiser and two escorts, a destroyer, and a frigate. The destroyer is turning; sensors indicate it is a missile class," said the tactical officer.

Clip and Jayneen had been able to use the galactic net, footage of the recent battles, and information from several different systems that had been in conflict with the Squilla in the last fifty years to gain information on Squilla ships, tactics, and tendencies in battle. Some of the information had been classified on system networks. Harmon did not feel guilty in the slightest when he asked for the information even though he knew how some of it would be retrieved.

"Bev, designate five missiles each on the battlecruiser and frigate. Ten for the missile destroyer. Lock them in and launch immediately," Harmon said. He wasn't taking any chances; a Squilla missile destroyer could pump out swarms of missiles.

"Clip, be ready down there," Harmon called down to the defensive bridge.

"We're as ready as we're going to be, man," Clip said. Harmon could hear the nerves in his voice.

"Missiles away and tracking, sir," weapons said.

"The battlecruiser has launched twelve fighters, sir," tactical said.

"Roger. Keep an eye on them, Adam," Harmon said.

"Flight deck. Fighters inbound. Launch all fighters," Clip said over all comms.

"The destroyer has launched twenty missiles," Jayneen said, down in the defensive bridge.

"One, fire a spread of eight shotgun missiles at the earliest interception point, programmed to detonate two seconds prior," Clip said to the Leethog occupying the first console.

"Yes, sir. Calculations complete. Launching," Defensive Position One said.

The hatches slid aside, and two groups of four defensive missiles fired off and turned toward the designated coordinates. Their rockets burned out eight seconds later. They were moving at an incredible speed and nearly invisible to enemy sensors. If the enemy's missiles stayed on target, they would meet the missile's shotgun blast.

Harmon watched the display on the main screen. He could see the three ships all turning toward them and the symbols indicating the inbound and outbound missiles. There was a circled area of the approximate spot the shotgun missiles would detonate. The outbound missiles passed the spot several seconds before the incoming missiles reached it, and they passed each other.

"Missile destroyer has launched another spread of twenty missiles, sir," tactical said. He knew the defensive bridge—the DB—was tracking it, but he wanted to inform the captain, as well.

Sixteen of the initial launch of Squilla missiles disappeared from the display. He could see the two escort ships pull ahead to provide cover for the battlecruiser. *Textbook,* thought Harmon. The symbols for the outbound missiles merged with the three Squilla ships. The defense lasers on *Salvage Title* engaged the four inbound missiles.

"Four missiles destroyed," Jayneen said down in DB.

"Sweet!" Clip exclaimed, clapping his hands and rubbing them together.

"Massive power surges on the frigate, sir. It's venting atmosphere and coming apart. There is slight damage to the missile destroyer and the battlecruiser," tactical said.

"Sir, we are within range of the main guns," weapons announced.

"Target that missile destroyer and fire at will," Harmon said.

The weapons officer fired all four cannons on that side as the ships were all coming together at an angle. Everyone on board felt the cannons fire one after another. Six seconds later, they felt them fire in the same sequence. It was repeated once more.

"Sir, the missile destroyer has broken apart. There is more damage indicated on the battlecruiser. It has fired eight missiles and is turning away," tactical let him know.

"DB, flight operations. All enemy fighters destroyed. We have two damaged fighters returning. No casualties. Do you wish to turn fighters over to TAC?" the flight officer asked.

"Roger that. Send them over," Clip said.

"TAC, flight operations. The fighters are yours," the flight officer said.

"Roger that," tactical replied. "Fighters will be in range of the battlecruiser in two minutes, sir."

"Bev, fire two more cannon salvos and cease fire," Harmon told weapons.

"Yes, sir," weapons answered.

"All fighters be advised. You will have zero friendly fire in one half mike, over," tactical said over the fighter comm network. "Engage with missiles when within range."

"Three. Fire one salvo of shotgun missiles," Clip said.

"Missiles away," Defense Position Three said.

"Abort. I am initiating abort on shotgun missiles. The fighters are in the path of the spread eight minutes out," Jayneen said.

"Fire a scrambler," Clip said.

A separate missile tube below the stern of the ship fired a jamming missile. From what Clip could figure out, it was designed to imitate the medium battlecruiser to any sensors and jam their guidance for oncoming missiles. There were only ten onboard, a rack of five loaded and five more stored in the small compartment where the tube was located. He didn't know if they would work on Squilla missiles since they had been made over twenty-two hundred years ago. He found out soon enough. It didn't work. The missiles continued toward them.

"Squat! Engage with all lasers, now!" Clip shouted.

All the lasers that could lock on began firing at their extreme range and continued as the missiles came in. One missile got through the crisscrossed pattern of fire and detonated against the shields. It was only one out of twenty-eight, but it was felt throughout the entire ship. Several circuit boards in the shield generators blew. Repair crews scrambled into action. They had to shut down those sections to fix them.

"Bridge, DB. We are down to ninety percent starboard shields. Not all of that was damage; we shut some of it down to fix it. Should be repaired in a few minutes," Clip called.

"Get them fixed. We have to catch the rest of them and see what we can do to help," Harmon replied.

* * *

Hank grinned as he reached up and fired four missiles at the flickering thrusters of the battlecruiser as he started to pass over from stern to bow. Other fighters also fired the last of their missiles. He kept his finger on the trigger of the lasers as the Squilla ship came apart. He was down to eighty percent shields from the dogfights. The Squilla fighters had been slower than the sleek fighter he was flying; it had been an exhilarating few minutes of dogfights.

"Bravo four, missiles away," he called over the squad network. He may have been an associate, but there was no way Harmon was letting the Leethog brothers be flight leaders. When they were on ship, it was one thing. When flying, they had to defer to experience. Hank didn't mind. He still had fun.

The fighters all pulled away as the fusion plants started to go in the battlecruiser, and it blew apart in a spectacular blast. Every Lee-thog in both squadrons had their helmet screen go dark momentarily. They flew back to the *Salvage Title* in formation.

"Tactical, get those fighters in. Helm, prepare to engage maximum thrust. Take us to the edge of the dampener's capability," Harmon directed.

"Zerith, we're going to have to push the engines. Any issues down there?" Harmon asked on comms.

"Power plant and engine room are ready to comply. I have been monitoring. Repair crewss are on sstandby," Zerith said. Harmon could swear he was eating something.

They had used twenty of the three hundred missiles they started with already. There were only two hundred and eighty still available. Harmon was worried they may not last through this battle. There was still twenty ships inbound toward the center of the system, and one was a Squilla Dreadnaught. He had tactical pull up the system view on the main screen, so he could see what the home fleet was doing and plan something. Anything.

* * *

Commander Three T'Kepta was still angry. *Rip Tide* and its escorts had been ordered to remain near the gate while the rest of the task force headed in system. The destruction of the rest of the human ships would result in several promotions. Promotions that he would not be receiving. It was a plot by K'Pitah to ensure a skilled commander did not rise in stature and challenge his right to command the task force, he was sure.

He would have to be promoted to command a heavy cruiser or one of the carriers by the high command before he could distinguish himself there and be considered a candidate for task force command. If he never had a chance to earn the right to a promotion to a bigger ship, then he couldn't challenge for the task force command position. It was deliberate.

T'Kepta was contemplating the assassination of the Task Force Commander One. He was sure no one would suspect a three of being the mastermind behind the plot. He knew a seven or two that would be willing to see it done in return for future favors. Perhaps L'Captic, commander of the corvette *Tidal Wave*. T'Kepta would contact him and set up a discreet meeting upon return to their system. After this one was destroyed, of course. Without realizing the habit, his small claw reached up and wiped his bulging eye while he was tapping his big claw.

"Commander, we have an incoming ship," the tactical officer said.

T'Kepta rose up on all eight legs on his commander's platform. A merchant ship would provide some entertainment to the boredom of gate patrol. As the squadron commander, he would have first choice of any goods before distribution to the fleet. He would not limit himself to the percentage allotted, either. His ship, his rules. He turned his eyestalks to the screen.

"That is no merchant. Look at its speed. Inform the *Undertow* and *Rippled Sand*," T'Kepta said.

* * *

The commander of the missile destroyer *Rippled Sand* had already given the order to turn and intercept the ship that had appeared on sensors by the time he was contacted by the squadron commander. His tactical officer told him that he thought it was a medium battlecruiser, but it was giving off readings he had never seen before. J'Bitwa hadn't become a commander five by hesitating. He ordered the weapons officer to fire a full spread as soon as he had a firing solution.

"The battlecruiser has fired twenty missiles, commander," said the tactical officer.

"Prepare the rapid lasers. Weapons, where is my launch?" demanded J'Bitwa, slamming his big claw onto his platform.

"Launching now, sir," answered weapons.

* * *

The commander of the frigate *Undertow*, a newly-promoted commander six, ordered his ship into overwatch, mimicking the destroyer. He and his officers could see the inbound missiles coming, and he debated firing the four missiles loaded in the tubes or just waiting to see if the spread by the destroyer was going to be enough. If he saved his missiles, he could use them later as the enemy ship was breaking up and perhaps deliver the killing blow. He already had his eyestalks on commander five.

"Engage the oncoming missiles with the rapid lasers," he commanded.

When the inbound missiles reached the trio of ships, despite all the defensive lasers, the frigate took three hits. The first two missile impacts overloaded the shields and blew the generators completely. Its commander never knew this, though, as the third missile blew the small ship nearly in half.

* * *

Aboard the medium Squilla battlecruiser, T'Kepta watched as the two escort ships engaged the incoming missiles. He ordered his weapons officer to do the same. He was not particularly worried. The rapid lasers would destroy the missiles. The few made it past them would not penetrate the shields. It took many human missiles to do that, the Squilla fleet had learned.

"Launch fighters," he ordered, confident the barrage of missiles headed to the unknown ship would all but render it defenseless.

To his surprise, six of the twenty missiles inbound made it past the lasers. Three hit the frigate, destroying it. One hit the destroyer, knocking its forward shields out of commission and damaging the ship. Two missiles hit his forward shield. The shield held, but there was major damage to the shield generators responsible for that area. He ordered the helm to turn about. Without orders, his weapons officer fired a half of a salvo of missiles now that there was an aiming solution. He would have to keep an eyestalk on that one.

He watched on the screen as another flight of missiles left the *Rippled Sand* and then the beams of energy began pounding it. Four impacts hit the *Rippled Sand* as it was turning, and a few seconds later, four more tore it apart. He stared and began to know fear. Four more hit what was left of the ship; the last two came through the wreckage and washed up against the shields of his ship, knocking him from his platform. His tactical officer called out damage reports, and the lights flickered as the energy beams tore into *Rip Tide*. He would never be promoted to commander two.

* * * * *

Chapter Twenty-One

"Sir, a ship has emerged through the gate. It is *Salvage Title*," Lieutenant Camille Kinigsly said.

Lieutenant Kinigsly was the tactical officer for *Tretra's Pride*, the flagship for the entire Tretrayon Defense Fleet. She was speaking to her commander, Captain Wynton Arton, but with Fleet Commander Admiral Timerton on the bridge, it was for his ears as well.

"One ship? There are three Squilla ships guarding the gate. She better be an extremely lucky ship. They'll pound her into scrap before she gets very far in system," Captain Arton said, shaking his head.

"*Salvage Title?*" Admiral Timerton asked. He walked up beside his flagship commander. "Tomeral was told to keep it out of this system. What the hell is he doing back?"

"Sir, *Salvage Title* is moving at a speed that none of our ships can match. Not for any period of time, anyway. It appears as if she is attacking the Squilla," the tactical officer said.

"Put it on the screen," Admiral Timerton said. "Sorry, Wynton." In his excitement he had overstepped his bounds. The ship belonged to its commander.

"No apologies needed, sir. These are trying times," Captain Arton said.

Second and third fleet were preparing for an imminent attack by twenty Squilla ships moving at maximum speed toward the inhabited

177

portion of the system. They had a little over three days before the battle began. All of first fleet had been destroyed in another system except for one heavily-damaged ship that had limped back.

The screen brought up what the tactical officer could see. It showed the symbols for the ships at the far end of the system. It showed the missiles and the fighters of all involved. There were sensors placed throughout the system for occasions like this. In hindsight, many thought that there should have been defense platforms throughout the system instead.

They watched in real time as *Salvage Title* destroyed the squadron guarding the gate. They couldn't tell what weapon was used besides the missiles, but they saw the readings and could tell that the Squilla ships were completely dismantled. There were very few power readings from any of the enemy ships.

"Sir, the Squilla ships are sending distress signals from several life pods," the ship's communications officer said.

"Get me *Salvage Title*," Admiral Timerton said.

* * *

"Sir, *Tretra's Pride* is hailing us," Lieutenant Jimtilnapray said, looking back at Harmon.

Here we go, he thought. "Put it on screen, Jim," Harmon said.

"Lieutenant Tomeral, I don't recognize that uniform, but I see you are wearing captain's rank," Admiral Timerton said.

"Yes, sir. It goes with the territory," Harmon said.

"Are you aware that we have activated the Inactive Reserve, Lieutenant?" Admiral Timerton said.

"I saw that. It looks like it happened a little over a week ago. I'm sure you are aware that the regulations state that if an IR member doesn't answer the call to duty within one week, it is assumed that they resigned from the Inactive Reserves and they are discharged," Harmon said.

"I see," Admiral Timerton said, looking off to the side. Harmon knew he was looking for verification.

"I may no longer be a member of the fleet, but this ship and I will be fighting for Joth. This means we would like to be included in any battle plans that you have for the system's defense," Harmon said, knowing he may be pushing his luck with the fleet commander.

Admiral Timerton looked back over to the side and his demeanor changed. He got his answer, and he didn't like it but was resigned. He looked back at the screen.

"Captain Tomeral, I am not sure what type of weaponry that ship has, but I just saw it tear apart a Squilla squadron. How about we let bygones be bygones and start fresh. I'll be honest with you; we need all the help we can get. The Squilla wiped out first fleet. Rear Admiral Cothco and his people gave it all they had, but in the end, it wasn't enough. The Squilla ships inbound are part of the fleet that destroyed him. I suspect that the other thirty ships will be here in a second wave inside of a week once they resupply," Admiral Timerton said.

"Sir, we're here to fight. What is your plan?" Harmon asked.

"I intend to send third fleet out around Joth and time it so the inbound will meet second head on while third hits its flank," Admiral Timerton said.

It was a solid plan, but it was predictable. Harmon thought for a moment and came up with an idea. Perhaps it would work. He decided to see it if the fleet commander would bite.

"Sir, that is a good plan, but isn't it one that the Squilla would be prepared for?" Harmon asked.

"What else can we do? That fleet has a dreadnought leading the charge," Admiral Timerton said, a little testily.

"Sir, if you would. Have your fleets both swing wide and come in at an angle at the point you can meet the Squilla. It may make them split their fleet. To take the system, they have to destroy the entire Tretrayon fleet. They won't continue straight for Tretra and risk you hitting both flanks. I will hit them hard from behind and take out as many as I can. I'm sure that by now they know what happened to their squadron. Maybe they will turn a few ships to meet me," Harmon said. "And we won't be directly behind the target when your ships fire. I am not interested in catching a stray missile or laser shots."

Admiral Timerton looked thoughtful. "So, you think catching them in an X attack may cause them to split? Interesting. We have time to swing out pretty far. Maybe they will split their fleet. We'll send you the coordinates of where the X will cross after we crunch the numbers based on their speed and ours," Admiral Timerton said.

"Sir, may I suggest that you attach a missile frigate to each of your light cruisers? They can attach underneath like they would for gate passage. It would give those ships a lot more firepower. That many missiles coming from a light cruiser will confuse their commander. They probably have a good idea of the ships remaining in system, but I don't think they have the sensor reach to make out individual ships yet," Harmon said.

"I like it. It will beef up those three ships. They can coordinate their shielding for added strength, too," Admiral Timerton said, impressed.

"Sir, we will be in range of the Squilla in time for the X to start crossing. We will attempt to hit the dreadnaught. If you would send that information over, I will have my lieutenant commander run over the numbers, and we'll set our speed accordingly," Harmon said.

"You mean have them run them through a computer? Absolutely. It shouldn't take long out here," Admiral Timerton said.

"No sir, my lieutenant commander will run the numbers herself. She won't need a navigation computer," Harmon said. He signed off immediately after saying this.

"You know you just confused the squat out of him," Clip said.

"Yep, I know," Harmon said. "You ready for this?"

"We'll be ready. We're trying to figure out if we can get the scrambler missiles to confuse the Squilla's technology. We tried it, but it didn't work. I don't think I have enough time to reprogram it, even with Jayneen's help. If I had that much knowledge of the Squilla's technology, I'd hack their ships and get them to shoot each other," Clip said with a grin.

"It would make life easier," Harmon said.

* * * * *

Chapter Twenty-Two

"We'll be within missile range in five minutes, sir," the ship's tactical officer said.

"Thanks, Adam," Harmon replied.

"Battle stations...All hands battle stations," Harmon announced over the ship's comm system.

"Four ships turned and are now heading to meet us. It looks like a heavy cruiser, a light cruiser, and two destroyers," the tactical officer said.

They had been chasing the Squilla fleet for almost three days. The Squilla commander was no fool; he had seen the ship's capabilities when it engaged his gate guards. He sent the squadron around early enough for them to have time to engage. He could not have them just turn around; it would have taken too long to slow down after performing the turnover maneuver and begin reverse thrusting. It would have put the ships at a major disadvantage with speed and maneuvering.

"They have launched...all four ships, a total of fifty-six missiles incoming," the tactical officer said, looking back at Harmon.

Down in the DB, Jayneen announced the incoming missiles at the same time to the room.

"One, fire a spread of twenty-four shotgun missiles. Have them detonate two seconds prior to the meet point," Clip said.

"Roger, sir," defense position one said. "Missiles away."

"Get the next batch ready. They'll fire another salvo shortly," Clip said.

"Launch a full spread of missiles. Target the destroyers. They are going to start pumping out missiles like there is no end to them, Bev," Harmon said to the weapons officer.

"Roger, sir. Missiles outbound," she said. "We can fire another round before we get within main gun range."

"Do it as soon as the tubes are loaded. Target the light cruiser with them," Harmon said.

"Helm, can you give us a little angle, so we can bring more cannons into the volley?" Harmon asked.

"Yes, sir. At least two more," the pilot answered.

"Wait, belay that. Here's what we will do," Harmon said, standing up. He had an idea.

"Zerith. You got me?" Harmon called back to the power plant on speaker, so the bridge crew could hear the plan.

"Yess, I am here," Zerith answered.

"Are you eating again?" Harmon asked, amazed. "Never mind, I know the answer. Look, I want to run something by you. Can we cut all thrust and perform half of the turnaround maneuver as if we were going to reverse thrust, but stop halfway?"

"We can, it sshould be no problem. We will be flying ssidewayss with our flank exxpossed to the enemy, and we will losse forward thrusst for that time," Zerith said, perplexed.

"Can we do it repeatedly?" Harmon asked, getting excited.

"Yesssss," Zerith said. Even for him, he stretched out the answer.

"Great. After we fire this salvo of missiles, I am going to direct helm to start the turnaround. We will cut thrust and stop halfway, then halfway, complete turnaround, and then continue...doing that." Harmon said.

"You intend to sspin the sship long enough to fire the cannonss from each position," Zerith said. "Nicce."

"Clip, will that keep you from using the defense lasers?" Harmon asked.

"No, they are positioned over the entire ship. Let me just say that this may be the craziest thing I have ever heard you say, and I have heard a lot. We're going to go spinning into battle. I am on a ship of fools," Clip declared.

"I think it will work," Jayneen said.

"You're encouraging this? Really?" Clip asked.

"That's what I'm talking about, Jayneen! Positive thinking, keep it up!" Harmon said. "Get ready."

"The destroyers have launched another spread of forty missiles," tactical announced.

"Launching twenty, sir," weapons said immediately after.

"Fire forward cannons and start the turns," Harmon said, strapping in.

"Launch a spread of twelve shotgun missiles," Clip ordered as he felt the cannons fire. The ship began turning.

The shotgun missiles detonated, sending their pattern of steel pellets toward the incoming missiles. Of the initial fifty-six, only eight made it through.

Clip ordered the defensive lasers to fire at extreme range.

The first volley of missiles from *Salvage Title* met the two destroyers. The destroyers' repeating lasers had destroyed sixteen of them before they reached the ships. One hit the lead destroyer, overloading its forward shields and causing some damage. Three missiles met the second destroyer. There had been a malfunction with some of its repeating lasers. It was a bad time for a relay to burn out. The first missile overloaded the shield. The next two missiles' warheads, with their shaped charges, penetrated deeply into the ship and exploded. It could still maneuver, but all missile tubes were offline with no hope of repair without a shipyard. It started to turn away.

Two missiles made it past the defensive lasers of *Salvage Title* and struck the port side shield and rocked the entire ship. The shields held, but several boards burned out. All four cannons on that side fired in order, and the ship turned again.

"Port shields down to eighty percent. Repair crews are working on them," Clip called up to the bridge.

The next salvo of shotgun missiles detonated, taking out thirty of the next incoming volley. The defensive lasers continued to fire their crisscrossed pattern.

The next twenty missiles were aimed at the heavy cruiser. The ship's repeating lasers were able to destroy eighteen of them. Its shield barely held. The heavy cruiser started turning to keep from getting hit there again.

The first two energy blasts from *Salvage Title*'s cannons ripped longitudinally through the first destroyer. One of the blasts hit a magazine, and it detonated, finishing the ship. The mounts retargeted on the light cruiser and pounded its shields. The next four tore through them and began ripping the ship apart. The rounds kept coming in, and it wasn't long before a blast went through the ship and hit the fleeing destroyer trying to hide behind it. The ship blew up with a spectacular blast. The engagement was now down to the heavy cruiser and *Salvage Title*.

Four missiles impacted against the *Salvage Title* and rocked it to its core. There was damage to the shields, and several other panels blew. The repair crews were busy putting out electrical fires all over the ship.

"Starboard shields are down to fifty percent. That was rough; we're doing what we can," Clip called up.

The pulse cannons continued to fire on the heavy cruiser as it attempted to turn away. It was destroyed before it could bring its main guns to bear on *Salvage Title*. The Squilla had several powerful lasers that could cause major damage, but they were weapons that required the ship to close in on an enemy. Harmon never let them get that close.

* * *

Aboard *Violent Seas*, Commander Two N'Litoh rose up on all eight legs on his commander's platform and ordered all ships to fire missiles. He nodded his eye stalks in satisfaction as fifty-six missiles streaked out from his heavy squadron.

He had seen the information on the devastation the lone ship had caused on the light squadron left to guard the gate. It should have been a simpleton's task. He did not know the commander of that squadron but was convinced it had to have been the worst three who had ever commanded. It would not happen to his squadron. There was a reason he was next in line to command a full fleet. Hesitation was not it.

"Incoming missiles," his tactical officer said. "Twenty."

"That's it?" scoffed N'Litoh. This would be over soon. He watched the screen and was surprised to see so many of his missiles detonate or go spinning off before they ever reached their target.

"What just happened?" he demanded, pounding his big claw.

"They were met by some defensive weapon. We were not tracking anything," the tactical officer said.

"The destroyers have launched a second volley," tactical said, shortly after.

"Good," answered N'Litoh.

"The enemy has launched twenty more and appears to be turning," tactical said.

"They are running, the cowards," N'Litoh said, settling back onto his platform.

He watched in horror as four missiles made it past all the repeating lasers and struck the destroyers. He had launched first, yet their missiles reached his ship before his reached theirs. One missile blew against *Ocean's Revenge*, and its shields flared and winked out. It began turning. Three missiles hit *Hidden Depth*, and two of them exploded within it.

He stood up on all eight legs again and heard the commander of *Ocean's Revenge* calling about electrical fires and repairing the weapons console. Energy blasts destroyed *Ocean's Revenge* before they could get their shields back, and then began hitting the light cruiser, *Shell Crusher*. Two blasts hit its forward shield, causing it to flare a light blue with waves rippling across it. Whatever was hitting it was powerful. The next four literally tore the ship to pieces.

Several of the next wave of energy blasts went through the wreckage of the light cruiser and struck the fleeing destroyer. It wasn't long before the weapon was turned on *Violent Seas*.

The communications officer on his ship had just enough time to send the information and the video footage to the task force commander before the bridge of the heavy cruiser blew apart with most of the ship.

* * *

"Zerith, talk to me. How are the plants holding up?" Harmon asked.

"He is busy with Kylatilaarnot. There was a fluctuation in fusion plant three. How may I help you, sir?" Vera asked.

Harmon was surprised to hear Vera in the power plant and not in the engine room. "Hey Vera, let them both know that I am about to ask the helm to push it to the limit. We have a timeline to make. Can the engines take it?"

"It is not good to push them to the red line for too long, but I understand that we have no choice. They are as ready as they can be," Vera said.

"Helm, push it. We have to make those coordinates on time," Harmon ordered.

Salvage Title headed in-system to the designated area to join the battle. As they chased the Squilla fleet, repairs were being made to the shields. They would need every bit of protection they could get. There were sixteen ships in the Squilla fleet, and one of them was a dreadnought, a ship nearly twice the size of *Salvage Title*.

* * * * *

Chapter Twenty-Three

"*Tretra's Pride. Salvage Title*," the comms officer called the flagship.

"Captain Tomeral," Admiral Timerton said as he appeared on screen.

"Sir, we will be in range to engage in six hours. From what we can see, the timeline is holding. It appears to us as if the Squilla have split their forces. The dreadnought is still headed straight in," Harmon said.

"It is. Intel says it is escorted by two destroyers and a carrier. It doesn't look like a fighter carrier, either. It looks as if they intend to put troops on the surface of Tretra. I have second fleet hitting their port side and third hitting starboard. I had the three beefed-up light battlecruisers, the flagship, and its escorts in reserve; they are no longer in reserve. I just gave orders for us to meet and come in at a slight angle of the dreadnought. We can't afford to leave anything in reserve," Admiral Timerton said. "We have to stop them here and then worry about the second wave that will be in system in a week."

"Sir, may I make a suggestion?" Harmon asked.

"By all means," Admiral Timerton said. "Your advice has been solid; we made a big mistake by not commissioning you years ago. Rest assured, there will be changes made after this war has been concluded. If I survive, that is,"

"There won't be much in-ship fighting, if any, today. Send your Marines, their mechs, and equipment to Tretra. If that carrier makes

191

it through to the surface, it'll be frost hunting them down. The Squilla have those single passenger tanks. They aren't as mobile as a mech, but they pack a frost of a punch. I don't know how many troops they can put on the ground, but one is too many. The ground defense forces are going to need all the help they can get," Harmon said.

"You're right. I can afford to send about half of them. The rest will have repair crew duty on the ships," he said. "The fleet has its orders. We'll meet after it's over. I'd like you to be in the meeting to plan for the next wave if we survive this one."

"I'll be there, sir. *Salvage Title* out," Harmon said, cutting the call. He settled back and waited on reports of the repairs. They would need all the shielding they could get.

* * *

The battle began when the Squilla missile carrier launched its first salvo, which was met with Tretrayon anti-missile missiles. Mixed in with the group were jamming missiles, and this time they actually had an effect on the Squilla missiles. The two sides closed in on each other as missiles flew. Fighters were launched, and before long, it was as chaotic a space battle that has ever been recorded.

There were three separate fronts with *Salvage Title* chasing down the dreadnought and its escorts.

"Fire a full spread at the dreadnought," Harmon ordered.

"Missiles away," weapons said.

"Clip, hand the fighters off to tactical. I want to send them after that carrier, before it turns loose its dropships," Harmon said.

"Alright, but if that dreadnaught launches fighters against us, our guys will be outnumbered at least two to one," Clip answered.

"I know. I'm banking on them slipping by," Harmon responded.

"Sir, the destroyers have launched missiles. It looks as if they are headed away toward the flagship," tactical said.

"We will be within main weapons range in two minutes, sir," weapons said.

"We can't afford to cut thrusters. Fire the forward cannons as soon as the banks charge, and don't stop. If we get that dreadnought, maybe we can take some of the resolve out of the commanders across their task force," Harmon said.

The pulse cannons began firing. One after another, they fired with a nine second gap between them. Harmon continued to order missile launches, and they got off three volleys with the forward cannons. The last one was aimed at one of the destroyers before they were able to turn and use the port cannons.

Clip used eight more salvos of the shotgun missiles to try to defeat the Squilla missiles that were aimed at them. When it was all said and done, the ship had taken enough missile strikes to bring the forward shield down to thirty-five percent. The repair crews were scrambling to fix the shield generators.

The energy blasts finally got through the dreadnought's shielding and began to wreak havoc on the ship. Unfortunately, it was after the dreadnought and its escorts had destroyed *Tretra's Pride's* escorts and two of the light carriers. The troop carrier didn't make it to Tretra, but it wasn't for lack of trying. It did manage to release four dropships, but they were taken out by a combination of Tretrayon fighters and the sleek fighters from *Salvage Title*.

Four Squilla ship commanders broadcast their equivalent of the white flag. Tretrayon Marines boarded their damaged ships and began shuttling the personnel to one of the remaining Tretrayon frigates. From there, they would take them to Tretra to place them in makeshift holding cells.

The flagship, *Tretra's Pride*, was running on one fusion plant and about one quarter of its engine power. One third of its crew did not survive the battle. Harmon invited the admiral and his surviving staff to *Salvage Title* to plan for the next wave. There was no way it could be held on the flagship.

* * *

Aboard the Squilla dreadnought, *Rogue Wave*, Commander One K'Pitah was watching the video of the unknown battlecruiser tearing through a heavy squadron with his second in command in charge. He didn't know if it was crewed by humans or their allies, but, in the end, it didn't matter. That ship was more than enough to give the humans the advantage, regardless of his task force's shielding and advanced missiles.

If he could just get Squilla on the surface of the capital planet, he could make these humans beg for peace...and then destroy them anyway. As his task force raced toward the center of the system, he prepared a report to send back through the gate. He would let the king know what they faced with that ship. If he failed, there would be more task forces following. Even if King C'Rabi had to pull ships from some of the systems they had subjugated, they would take this system.

"The battlecruiser has fired missiles on us," the tactical officer said.

"Engage with rapid lasers. Launch missiles on those ahead of us. We must get to the planet," K'Pitah ordered.

The lasers stopped eighteen missiles. When the two remaining missiles hit the rear shields, it rocked the dreadnought, even as big as it was. K'Pitah felt it through his platform. When the energy blasts started hitting the shield, he knew they would not reach the planet.

"Sir, the light cruisers ahead have just launched thirty-two missiles each. Ninety-six missiles are inbound, and all of them are targeting *Rogue Wave*," tactical told him. His eyestalks were dropping in resignation. "We have miscalculated their capabilities. We should have concentrated on them first. They will be able to launch again before we can target them."

He was still receiving damage reports when the bridge was breached, and he was pulled through the hole and into space.

* * * * *

Chapter Twenty-Four

Five shuttles sat in the bay of *Salvage Title*. Admiral Timerton, Captain Arton, Jr. Captain Opawn, Commanders Largoss and Allen, and Captain Loid were seated in the conference room off the bridge of the ship. The original crew of *Hauler* was seated there as well. Lieutenant General Wilton was present through a video call, as was Jayneen, though there was no image of her. That was an ace in the hole that Harmon wasn't ready to reveal to the entire universe yet.

"The capabilities of this ship are impressive, as is the crew. I cannot believe you were able to hire fully-trained personnel," Admiral Timerton said. "Can I say personnel? They are Leethog, are they not?"

"You can, sir. It translates to something acceptable to them. I prefer to call them beings like we call everyone on Joth," Harmon said. "If it wasn't acceptable, I am sure they would let you know. Especially our chief warrant officer," Harmon said, indicating the smallest being in the room.

All heads turned toward Kyla, who smiled. Introductions had been made around the room, but her smile still obviously unnerved some of the Tretrayon officers. Big Jon, leaning against the wall behind Harmon, hissed as he laughed to himself.

"I thought all Leethog were...small. Your bodyguard isn't so small, and he carries himself as well as any Marine," Lieutenant General Wilton said through the video link. He had realized he had amends to make.

"Staff Sergeant Jontilictick is in charge of the ship's security. He is not necessarily my bodyguard, sir. And yes, he is one being that handles himself well. If the Squilla make it to the planet, I intend to send him and his platoon down to help in the fight," Harmon said.

"We need to formulate a plan," Admiral Timerton said, bringing the subject back to the reason for the meeting. "We have about one week before thirty more Squilla ships come through the gate. We only have seven ships, eight counting this one. And *Tretra's Pride* is in bad shape. My engineer says she can get us another fusion plant and half engine power within five days, but that's it."

"Well, sir, we have been discussing it. We think we have something," Harmon said.

"I'm all ears," Admiral Timerton said.

Hank and Stan started hissing, poking each other, and looking at the admiral. Vera whistled for them to stop, and they just kept laughing. Even Big Jon was laughing again. Kyla hissed, and all three of them stopped immediately.

"What did I say?" Admiral Timerton asked.

Kyla sighed and said, "They are laughing because humans have very little ears, sir," she said, giving the three male Leethog in the room a look. "It was rude, and I apologize for them."

"They are males," Vera added, looking over to Jr. Captain Opawn, as if she could sympathize. Opawn hid her smile.

Admiral Timerton smiled, reached up, and rubbed his ear. He was not upset; he understood combat humor. When all hell was about to break loose, it was often how members of the fleet coped. Perhaps it was the same with other races.

"We think that we can get several of the fleet ships' fusion plants started to provide enough power for their weapons. We will have to tow them into place, but they can be a surprise for the Squilla," Harmon said.

"We could link their computers remotely to one source so we don't have to have anyone aboard the hulls. Environmental, main engines, none of that will be necessary," Clip said.

"That would have to be a pretty powerful computer. I don't think the flagship could handle it," Captain Arton said.

"Clip can program them. I can handle it," Jayneen said.

"I? You mean you have a computer on this ship that can handle it?" Admiral Timerton asked.

"Tell them," Zerith said.

"Yes, tell them," Jayneen said.

Harmon looked around the room. Every Leethog was nodding its head. Clip just shrugged. If his friend wanted it to be known, then he agreed with her.

"Lieutenant Commander Jayneen…is an AI," Harmon said. "Sorry Jayneen, I know you are not artificial," he added.

"I understand. It is so they can understand what you are saying, but don't make a habit of it," Jayneen said.

The room was silent as the members of the Tretrayon fleet realized what Captain Tomeral was saying. He couldn't blame them. It was a lot to grasp. There were races with very powerful computers, but there was no known example of the ever-elusive artificial intelligence.

"Amazing. I had no idea, as we were talking to you," Admiral Timerton finally said. "You can control all the weapons on the ships we put together?"

"I can, but like any other being, I have my shortcomings. I will need Harmon to give me instructions. I am self-aware and capable of independent thought. However, I am a lousy tactician. I lack the instinct for battle. In that regard, I am just like any other being. I need guidance, training, and experience. Not everyone has the ability to do what Harmon has done," Jayneen said.

"If you already realize that, you can become a leader one day. You can't be a leader if you are unable to take orders yourself, lieutenant commander," Lieutenant General Wilton said.

"Why don't we use the Squilla ships in the same manner?" Kyla asked the room.

"If I had access to their systems, I could figure it out," Clip said.

"We could park them close to the gate," Harmon said.

"And fire everything they have at the Squilla as they go by, whittling them down before we have to face them with what is left of our fleet," Admiral Timerton said. "I like it."

"I suggest we bring every Marine to Tretra. If their plan is still the same, they will try to land troops on Tretra," the Marine commander said. "Even with the ground defense, we will need all the help we can get."

"If they land on Joth, they won't make it very far. Everyone iss armed," Zerith said.

"Unfortunately, on Tretra, only the military and law enforcement are armed," said Lieutenant General Wilton.

Over the next three days, repair crews worked around the clock to repair what they could on the disabled fleet ships. Clip wrote a program that would allow remote usage of the weapons consoles. Several intel officers expressed their dismay that he was able to do it.

Not just quickly...but do it at all. Admiral Timerton sent word through the fleet for those voices to shut the hell up.

Missile tubes and racks were reloaded on the ships they were able to restore some power to. Several ships' bridges were destroyed. Zerith came up with a work-around for those ships—a simple slate wired directly into the launchers with minimal targeting programs. Basically, the missiles were going to be fired out of their tubes and would lock onto the nearest signature that was larger than a missile rocket engine.

Salvage Title raced out toward the gate with the four Squilla ships attached. In space, aerodynamics do not matter, so the ridiculous shape of the ungainly collection was not slowed by it as they headed out. Three frigates and a destroyer had survived the battle, since second and third fleet initially targeted the larger ships. Their commanders had surrendered before they could be destroyed. The destroyer was a missile ship, and it still had enough missiles for four full volleys.

As soon as Clip finished the program and sent it encrypted through the net to fleet, he started figuring out how to do the same thing with the Squilla ships. With the time restraints, he opted to write a patch that put the helm and weapons consoles on remote operations. They were detached and sent in a patrolling pattern off to the side of the gate. Before they detached, Clip had the shuttle fly to the front of the destroyer, and Hank and Stan suited up and used a sealant to attach twelve shotgun missiles to the hull of the ship. They could be remotely detonated.

By the time *Salvage Title* got back to the area of the battle, six days had passed. Fleet personnel had managed to restore eight ships enough that they could launch missiles. Two more ships had been repaired enough so they could place crews on them and actually fight. The personnel came from those they rescued from damaged ships and life pods.

All in all, there were four Squilla ships out near the gate, as well as eight weapons platforms and nine functional fleet ships. Along with *Salvage Title*, it would have to do. All the fleet ships had full missile loads after they pulled them from the ships they didn't have time to repair. The fleet moved deeper into the system so the Squilla would have to come past the platforms to meet them.

* * * * *

Chapter Twenty-Five

Two days later, the Squilla arrived. They came through the gate in squadrons, one after another. There were thirty-one ships. They were nearly at their maximum speed and headed straight for Tretra.

"We have an emergence," Jayneen announced over the entire fleet's comms. It would take almost four days before they reached the planet. Jayneen waited until all of the ships came through and then launched a total of thirty-two missiles at the destroyers in the third and fourth squadrons. Twenty missiles from the captured destroyer went to one squadron and twelve from the frigates at another. She also fired all four ships' pulse lasers at a light cruiser in the fourth squadron as well.

The first Squilla destroyer targeted was able to stop fourteen missiles before the rest impacted. Six made it past the ship's rapid laser defense. The last missile impacted deeply enough in the ship that it started a chain reaction in the missile magazines, and it blew apart. The destroyer was followed so closely by the squadron behind it that some of the debris hit the forward shield of one of its frigates.

The next destroyer targeted stopped ten missiles. The two missiles that hit rocked the ship and left its shields weak. The pulse lasers, all aimed at the light cruiser, burned through its shields and hit the ship near its engines.

The second Squilla destroyer was able to fire a full spread back at the now-Tretrayon destroyer. Jayneen blew the shotgun missiles, and they destroyed eighteen of the twenty incoming missiles. She launched another round from all four ships. Twelve missiles from the frigates went to the offending destroyer, and two of them slammed into the ship, heavily damaging it and destroying its usefulness for the upcoming battle. The twenty missiles from the destroyer were aimed near the engines of the light cruiser, and three made it through the ship's defenses. The aft end of the ship separated from the hull as its power plants blew.

By this time, the shock of the unexpected attack was over, and missiles came in from most of the incoming task force. All four ships were destroyed in the onslaught but not before the pulse lasers destroyed the frigate that had been damaged when the first destroyer blew up. The Squilla were down to twenty-seven ships.

* * *

Supreme Commander One L'Kivil was on his platform in the mega-dreadnought *Tidal Wave*, the largest of all Squilla ships. The king had sent him to personally wipe out the defending fleet of the Tretrayon System. The reports of the first wave's battle had reached them through the gates. Most of what had been written was probably lies to make up for mistakes and the failure to take the system. He would prove it to the king himself. It was ridiculous; a member of the high command had to oversee the destruction of an out-of-the-way inferior system. He had better things to do than this. He had wives waiting in his lagoon for him. *Just ridiculous*, he thought.

Tidal Wave led the task force. He would have no other ship ahead of him. Lessons were to be learned. L'Kivil was looking at the main screen with both eyestalks as they came through the gate. Sensors showed the wreckage of three Squilla ships near the gate. And there, on the other side, was a light squadron of Squilla ships moving toward the gate, as if they were on gate guard.

Perhaps the reports sent back had been hasty, he thought. Farther in system, the sensors indicated numerous wrecks and powerless hulls. Some showed minor power fluctuations, which was to be expected after a major battle. There were many more that showed no energy readings whatsoever.

"Sir, we detect a light squadron nearby. It is the destroyer *Whitecap* and three escorting frigates. They are moving in overwatch pattern Lima," the tactical officer informed him. "Evidence of three destroyed ships are farther from the gate. There are indications that a major battle took place much farther in system."

"Can you locate the rest of the task force? How far away are they?" L'Kivil demanded. He could already see what he had just been told.

If there was a light squadron guarding the gate, then the idiots must have finally succeeded in taking the system. *If I made this trip for no reason, claws will roll*, he thought. He relaxed and eased back down onto his commander's platform.

"Incoming!" the tactical officer shouted. "*Whitecap* and its escorts have launched missiles...directly at third and fourth squadrons!"

"What?" L'Kivil sprang up on his legs. "Hail them now!" he shouted. It had to be a mistake; they needed to self-destruct the missiles now. *Idiots!*

"Incoming! Twenty missiles inbound! Sir, *Whitecap* has fired on us!" the tactical officer of the destroyer *Hidden Reef* shouted over the radio.

"Use anti-missile defense delta…no use bravo! What the chum are they thinking?!" L'Kivil shouted back.

The defensive lasers stopped just fourteen of the incoming missiles. It had been a surprise, and the hesitation cost them. Six missiles impacted against the shields on *Hidden Reef's* flank. The shields couldn't hold, and the last missile impacted deep enough to set off an entire missile rack. The ship exploded, sending debris in every direction. A large piece crashed into the frigate *Driftwood* and knocked out most of its shielding.

Twelve missiles were aimed at the destroyer *Poison Barb* from the three frigates. Its crew was able to stop ten of them, but the last two rocked the ship and left it with fifteen percent shields on that side. His ship fired a spread of twenty missiles back at *Whitecap* even though L'Kivil hadn't ordered it. He then watched in shock as eighteen of the outbound missiles either blew apart or went careening off in different directions. Two missiles impacted, buckling the shields of the traitorous ship but did not do any major damage.

"The lasers from those ships are hitting us!" the tactical officer on the light battlecruiser *Strangling Kelp* called. "They're going to overload our shields! They are at seventy-five percent and dropping quickly!"

L'Kivil's tactical officer cried out, "There are twenty missiles inbound toward *Strangling Kelp!*"

"Engage with the rapid lasers!" L'Kivil shouted, coming off his platform toward the main screen. He couldn't believe this was happening.

Three missiles made it through the defense and impacted in the power plant and engine areas. One quarter of the ship was blown off, and the light cruiser went spinning out of control.

L'Kivil looked at his screen and saw they were headed toward *Poison Barb,* whose shields were fluctuating between twelve and eighteen. "Twelve more missiles, incoming!" L'Kivil's tactical officer cried out.

The ship's defense lasers fired their crisscrossing pattern, and only two missiles made it through the laser fencing to slam into the ship. "The *Poison Barb* is reporting fires in almost every major console and penetration in six decks," he added. "Their power plant initiated an automatic shutdown, and they are running on emergency power. They have enough power to sustain the environmental systems for five days. Maybe six."

"Fire!" L'Kivil yelled. "All ships fire on the traitors!"

Sixteen of the remaining Squilla ships launched missiles at the renegade ships, but they were too late to keep the traitors' lasers from striking the frigate *Driftwood* several times each. Its shields fell, it was cut open, and most of its crew were exposed to the vacuum of space.

L'Kivil was livid. Four ships of his task force had been destroyed or rendered combat ineffective. Four. He ordered his crew to scan for any more ships near them, Squilla or human. He would not be lulled into another trap.

His tactical officer assured him the only active ships were three days away, and there were only ten of them. One was of an unknown design, but it was only the size of a medium battlecruiser. It was the ship that had given the first task force so much trouble, as identified by its strange sensor readings.

"Increase speed," L'Kivil ordered to his entire task force.

* * *

"**G**reat job, Jayneen," Harmon said.

"It was exhilarating, though a part of me is sad to have used those ships up like that. They are not aware, but I was linked into their computers for a time," Jayneen said.

"Well, get ready, because you have to control eight of them in about three days," Clip said.

"Yes, but those are just weapons platforms now. I don't have to move them," the AI said.

"Thiss iss true, but you will have many more missiless to keep track of," Zerith said.

"A lot of them will be fire and forget, coming from some of the ships with no bridges," Harmon said. "I want you to fire at the most extreme range you can and fire at them until you can't anymore. Take out their missile ships as soon as you can. If you get all of those, then lay it into that mega-dreadnought. They will retaliate, and there is little shielding on those wrecks, but you may be able to get off four full salvos." The AI started calculating the range.

* * * * *

Chapter Twenty-Six

"Sir, the Squilla will be in range in two hours," Harmon said. "Once our platforms start firing, the enemy won't be able to get out of the kill box. At the speed they're going, they can alter their course, but their momentum will still bring them all within range,"

"Good, we need to take as many out as we can before we meet them head on," Admiral Timerton said. "An hour after they come past those platforms, the entire fleet will be engaged. I have assigned *Vanot* to fly as escort for *Salvage Title*. It has its own weapons plus the missiles from *Tripton*."

"Outstanding, sir. It's going to be another surprise for them," Harmon said.

Two days ago, Zerith had casually walked onto the bridge and let Harmon know that he had an idea. He had explained, between bites of a green-and-red-striped apple, that they could lock a few of the ships with power plants beyond repair to the hulls of running ships. If they then ran power cables to the damaged ships, they ought to be able to get some weapons working and maybe even some shields, too. After working nonstop for two days, the four fleet ships now had the fire power of eight. Two of them had the capabilities to launch forty-eight missiles in one volley.

"We have the Marines on Tretra in case some of the dropships get through, which might happen. Several hours ago, a carrier peeled off from the rest and began swinging around toward the planet. We can't afford to send a ship after it. Your ship is the only one with the speed to intercept it, but that dreadnought is coming right down our throats," Admiral Timerton said.

"We could send fighters, sir," Harmon suggested.

"We could, but they would be out of fuel. We can't have them stranded in space somewhere, along with everything else that's going on."

Jayneen brought up all of the power plants at the same time. They had been powered down to the bare minimum to mask their energy readings. A little over one minute later, one hundred and sixteen missiles leapt out toward the incoming Squilla task force. They were a quarter of the way to their targets when another volley left their tubes. When the first rounds were halfway, one hundred more missiles flew out. One of the platforms had a power surge and did not respond to Jayneen's remote command.

By this time, the Squilla ships had launched missiles in return. Over four hundred missiles were headed in toward the ambush site. With the distance between the task force and the platforms shrinking, Jayneen was able to send one more wave of one hundred missiles before the damaged ships were shredded and unable to respond to her commands. The next wave of Squilla missiles was wasted on what was left of the makeshift defense platforms.

When the Squilla task force came through the wreckage of the ambush site, there were only eighteen ships still capable of fighting. Of four hundred and thirty-two missiles, forty-six had eluded the lasers and hit shields, and nine of those shields had been penetrated. Jayneen had concentrated on the missile ships, but other ships had been hit, too. The dreadnought was still leading the charge, but even its shields had been weakened.

* * *

L'Kivil saw the energy readings at the site of the last battle spike at the same time his tactical officer called it out. Four ships were still capable of providing power to their weapons. His ships were not in range to fire on them yet when over a hundred missiles were launched toward them. He could not order the launch because the missiles would go out away from his fleet toward stationary targets. Those same targets could launch at his task force because they were coming to the target. It was simple math. He slammed his big claw on the platform, in frustration.

"Sir, we cannot evade at this rate of speed, and the defense lasers will be less accurate because of the closing speeds of the incoming missiles," his tactical officer told him.

Minutes later, L'Kivil asked, "How many?"

"Four hundred and thirty-two missiles were launched at us. Several of our ships have been disabled," the tactical officer said. As he said it, the dreadnought shuddered as several missiles hit its forward shield.

"Forward shields down to eighty percent, sir. Our missiles are just now striking the targets. There appears to be little shielding. There will be no more missiles fired from there," his tactical officer said.

Aboard the large missile carrier *Undersea Volcano*, its commander watched as its rapid lasers went off in a never-ending wave. It was not enough. The entire ship jolted as the missiles hit the shields. He was still watching when two missiles, one after another, seemed to strike the clear-steel portals of the bridge…and blow it away.

* * *

"Three minutes until they are within range, sir," weapons said.

"Thanks, Bev," Harmon said. It was time. Either they would survive this battle, or it would mean the end to the system. The end to Joth, his home. He thought of Rinto and wondered what he was doing. Probably sitting behind a makeshift barricade, armed to the teeth in case the Squilla put troops on the planet. *Frost! Most of the planet probably had weapons in hand as they all waited on the results of this battle.*

The president of the system had made the invasion announcement thirty minutes ago, and it had been broadcast throughout the system. The beings of Joth were armed and ready. Tretra was a different matter; its population didn't have weapons. If the Squilla landed, it was going to be bad...really bad. He hoped Evelyn and her Marines were prepared.

"Missiles away," weapons announced.

"Incoming," tactical announced at the same time.

"Forty missiles inbound," Jayneen said in the DB.

"Forty! It has to be from the dreadnought. Position One, fire four groups of shotgun missiles. Time it for two seconds from crossing point," Clip said.

"Sixteen away," said the Leethog sitting at defense position one.

"The Squilla have launched fighters. It appears to be all they have available. Sensors indicate over four hundred fighters inbound," Jayneen said.

"Flight Deck. This is DB. Launch all fighters," Clip called down.

"Roger, launching all fighters," the flight officer confirmed.

"Thirty-two of the inbound missiles were stopped by the shotgun missiles," three said. "Engaging with lasers."

Two missiles hit the forward shields, bringing them noticeably down. The missiles the dreadnought were firing were more powerful than the ones that had preceded it. Too many more of those, and the ship would start taking real damage.

"Zerith, prepare for turnover maneuvers," Harmon called.

"We are ready, it sshould help sspread the impactss around the sshieldss, too," Zerith said.

"Firing forward main weapons," weapons announced.

"Helm, begin rotation," Harmon said.

Salvage Title started firing its cannons as it rotated, giving the banks of each pulse cannon time to recharge. All of its shots were aimed at the mega-dreadnought. The weapons officer continued to launch missiles as they were loaded into the tube.

Time seemed to slow as the ship shuddered, both from the cannons firing and the missiles impacting against the shields. Finally, a missile impacted against the side of the battlecruiser; the shields on that side had given way. Major damage was done to several decks, and two pulse cannons on that side were destroyed. Repair crews were scrambling. Fires were fought, compartments sealed against exposure to open space...and crew members died.

The damage happened on the opposite side of the ship from the flight deck, but several crew members were knocked away from the deck, and the only thing that saved them were the tethers attached to their suits. All of the fighters but the Zax had been launched. The flight officer ordered the bay door closed.

"Status report! Get me a report!" Harmon yelled as he climbed back into his seat. There was smoke coming from one of the consoles. It was shut down, and the junior engineering officer ran to the backup console and started calling out which decks were breached and which were just damaged.

"Adam, what's the status of the dreadnought?" Harmon asked over the sounds of alarms.

"It's damaged, sir! It's venting atmosphere and it is showing major power fluctuations. It has not fired any missiles in the last two minutes. Only one of its main lasers seems to be working, though it has missed us on its last three shots," tactical announced.

"Hit it again, Bev. Helm, keep that side away from them in case they fire again. Target missiles toward the heavy cruiser," Harmon ordered. He noticed the cruiser turning toward them, and felt like they might get the upper hand after all.

* * *

"Fire a full spread at that heavy cruiser," Captain Arton ordered. It was time to get into the battle; the enemy had come in range.

Admiral Timerton was observing from his station off to the side of the ship's commander. It was the captain's ship, and he did his best to let the ship's commander fight the ship as he saw fit. He noticed the symbols for fighters entering the fray as the ship's tactical officer said, "Admiral, the Squilla have launched over four hundred fighters."

"Get them all out, Wynton," he told Captain Arton.

"Tretrayon fleet," Captain Arton called. "Launch all fighters and engage the enemy fighters. I say again, launch all fighters."

Three hundred and eighty fighters launched from the fleet, the majority of which came from *Aganon*, the last remaining Tretrayon fighter carrier. It took several launch waves before they were all in space.

"Sir, the dreadnought has started coming apart. *Salvage Title* and *Vanot* went head to head with it. *Vanot* has lost most of its engines but continues to fire half salvos of missiles from *Tripton,* which is attached to it," the tactical officer of *Tretra's Pride* said. "All ships are engaging."

* * *

In *Salvage Title*'s power plant, Zerith had been frantically trying to keep Fusion Plant Three from initiating shutdown. Its temperatures were beyond the safety parameters. He did all he could and looked over at Kyla.

"Sshut it down. There iss nothing we can do," Zerith said.

"Yes, it is best," she agreed, nodding her head. There was a trickle of blood down one side of her face. She had been knocked into a console after a missile impact and had refused medical attention. *There was no quit in that race,* Zerith thought approvingly.

"Engineering to bridge. Initiating sshut down of Fussion Plant Three. There will be an additional three ssecondss added to the main guns' energy bank charging time," he called up.

"Roger that," the young engineer said. She informed tactical and weapons.

* * *

Across, over, below, and between the huge ships slugging it out, another battle was being fought. Fighters swooped, rolled, dodged, and jinked in space combat. The bulky Squilla fighters were slower and less maneuverable than the Tretrayon fighters and were even worse off against the sleek fighters from *Salvage Title*. This evened the odds, despite the numerical advantage the Squilla had. Additionally, whenever a Leethog saw an opening, they broke loose from the dogfights and fired missiles at the larger ship's engines below them.

Stan had just released the last of his missiles at a light cruiser when his fighter was raked with laser fire from a Squilla craft. He had already lost his rear shield, so the laser blasts destroyed the main engines in his fighter. He had the battery-powered maneuvering thrusters and comms, but not much else.

"This is Bravo Five. I have lost main engines," he called over the fighter channel. "I am initiating plant shutdown."

Stan shut down the power plant, and his fighter drifted. With the plant offline, the fighter didn't show up on other craft's sensors as a viable threat, and Stan hoped the Squilla fighter pilots wouldn't see it in the vastness of space and target it again. His encoded distress beacon activated automatically, and he sat, watched the flashes in the distance, and hoped the battle would end soon so he could restart the plant and the heater.

Thirty minutes later, he saw a shadow cross over the cockpit. Hank was looking at him upside down. He had matched Stan's drift and rotation. He grinned, waving down, and Stan waved up at his brother. Hank flipped his fighter and engaged the magnetic struts that locked it to the flight deck, and Stan felt the fighters come together. It was so cold in his fighter he couldn't feel his ears in the helmet. He started his power plant and wondered how the rest of the battle went.

* * *

Supreme Commander L'Kivil appeared on the screen on the bridge of the heavy troop carrier. "Commander Two W'Coltah, you will swing *Endless Krill* around and approach the home world of this system and send the dropships and all the claw soldiers to the planet. Shell Commander One N'Tikah, I want you to destroy the capital and make them sue for peace. I believe we will be victorious; we have almost twice as many ships as the humans, despite the cowardly ambushes, and we will support you from orbit. After this is over, I will await the decision from the king. We will either subjugate these humans or destroy them like the last system. If it were my decision, I would eradicate the species."

"Yes, sir," W'Coltah said.

"It will be done," N'Tikah said. He was dressed in a mottled mesh covering his shell, with vented armor over the soft, vital parts of his body. On his small claw, a laser rifle was strapped in place. He and his claw soldiers would be ready.

Five hours later, the fleets were in range of one another. L'Kivil had decided to take on the battlecruiser that had caused so much damage. Its readings were strange, and his tactical officer could find no reference to that class of ship other than the reports that had been sent from the skirmishes with his race's ships. The reports had to have been exaggerated; a medium battlecruiser could not do that much damage by itself. Even now, a light cruiser was flying overwatch. *How much damage could those two ships do?* he thought. *Tidal Wave* was much more powerful, even against their combined might.

"Launch missiles," he ordered.

"Missiles launched," weapons replied.

"Incoming," tactical said. "Twenty missiles are inbound from the strange ship, and forty-eight are coming from the light cruiser!" he shouted.

"What? From a light cruiser? That ship does not show to be a missile carrier," L'Kivil yelled. "Fire the main weapons!"

"We will not be in range for the main lasers for five minutes, sir," weapons answered reluctantly.

"Sir, thirty-two missiles from our salvo have been destroyed or went off course before they reached the ship's shields," the tactical officer said, perplexed, before being thrown from his position as two massive energy blasts rocked the forward shields, followed quickly by the explosions from the six missiles that had breached the rapid laser defense system. The smell of burning wires came from the ventilation system as some of the relays to the shield generators overloaded.

"Sir, forward shields down to sixty percent," tactical called out.

"Keep launching full salvos and fire the main lasers on the missile carrier when it comes in range," L'Kivil demanded.

Four more energy blasts pounded the forward shields, followed shortly after by two more. The rain of missiles seemed endless. Smoke covered the lower portion of the room; its acrid smell overloaded his senses.

Reports were coming in from the task force. They were taking missiles and shots from ships with twice the firepower their reports said they should have. Some of their shields seemed impenetrable.

"Launch all fighters!" he ordered, looking for any way to turn this around.

The heavy cruiser *Fourteen Seas* had maneuvered within range of the unknown battlecruiser and was preparing to fire when it was struck with missiles from the damaged human battlecruiser.

Tidal Wave refused to answer the helm's command, and Supreme Commander One L'Kivil knew it was hopeless. The artificial gravity began going in and out, and six of his legs had to grip onto the commander's platform to stay atop it. Damage reports were coming in, and the pounding was not stopping. *What type of weapon was that? What race has raw energy as a cannon round?* he asked to himself.

The flight leaders were reporting heavy losses. There were fighters they had never seen before outmaneuvering and outgunning them. They would not turn the tide of the battle.

L'Kivil knew the task force would not be providing orbital support for the claw soldiers, although they still had a chance because the system didn't have an abundance of ground warriors. They could take the capital and hold it until the king could put together another task force. *It could be pieced together and in-system within six months,* he thought, just before the ship exploded.

* * * * *

Chapter Twenty-Seven

The last Squilla ship surrendered. It was a light battle-cruiser that had lost its engines and was severely damaged. Admiral Timerton was surprised it could even send out a signal. Out of the entire Squilla task force, only three ships held any type of atmosphere. There were escape pods everywhere, but they were not all Squilla.

Of the ten ships that had defended the system, three ships were still moving under power. The medium battlecruiser *Brunner*, the fleet's flagship *Tretra's Pride*, and *Salvage Title*. There were ships with no power that still had living crew members, too.

"Get the shuttles moving; we have a lot of people to rescue," Admiral Timerton told Jr. Captain Opawn. She would handle the fleet rescue operations while her commander handled the repairs of *Tretra's Pride*.

"With *Aganon* out of commission, I'll have to land the fighters that are left wherever we can. Too bad these newer models can't operate in atmosphere. We could fuel them up and send them to Tretra," Jr. Captain Opawn replied.

"Sir, the Squilla troop carrier is just hours from Tretra's orbit," the tactical officer told Admiral Timerton.

"Hell, get me Tomeral," he responded.

* * *

"Cease fire, Bev. They're done," Harmon said.

"Yes, sir. Powering down the main guns," she answered, exhausted.

"Lena, move us away from the wreckage so we can get our fighters back. Someone give me the ship's status," he said. The pilot eased the ship out of the debris from the Squilla warship they'd just destroyed.

"We have sealed off decks five through seven. We lost two pulse cannons on the starboard side, and we are down to three fusion plants. Engines are at three quarters output. We have lost all shields on the starboard side. Rear shields are at twenty-two percent. Port shields are at fifty percent. Forward shields...are at only five percent," the bridge engineer finished reading, looking up with fear in her young eyes.

Harmon shook his head. *Salvage Title* had taken a beating. The forward shields were the strongest on the ship, and one more missile strike would have penetrated it. Possibly into the bridge itself.

"Thank you, Warrant Officer Saratileentrop," Harmon said. He knew she was still scared, but she had never left her post. *She had the makings of a fine officer*, he thought.

"Bridge to medical. Status?" Harmon called.

"Captain, we have eighteen killed in action. I have another four in critical condition and scores with minor wounds. Four are unaccounted for. The flight officer has informed me that two pilots perished, as well," the ship's doctor answered. She sounded as if she was in a hurry.

"Thanks, doc," Harmon said. *Twenty-four. Frost!* He wondered who the pilots were. Hopefully, not the brothers.

"Zerith, what does it look like down there?" he asked, calling down to engineering.

"It looks like a messs," Zerith said. "We had to sshut down the troublessome plant. There iss ssome damage to one of the enginess, and Vera and her crew are working on it, but they do not have the sspare partss they need. Kyla went to ssee if sshe could help."

"How are your folks?" Harmon asked him.

"They are tired, but they are determined," Zerith answered. "Minor injuriess, no losssess."

"Alright, do what you can," Harmon said.

"Call from *Tretra's Pride*, sir," the communications officer said.

"Put it on, please?" Harmon asked.

"Captain Tomeral, the Squilla troop carrier is just hours from Tretra. How soon can you be underway? Can you take it out before it starts releasing its dropships?" Admiral Timerton asked.

"We're at three quarters engine output. We can try, sir, but I can't guarantee it," Harmon said. "We'll get our fighters on board and redline it all the way in."

"You do that. We'll be following as fast as the *Pride* can go," Admiral Timerton told him, and he signed off.

"Zerith, clean us up as best as you can…we're going to have to redline it to the planet," Harmon called over the comms.

"Perhapss you sshould be the one to tell the little oness," Zerith said hesitantly.

"That's all you, friend…all you," Harmon replied.

"Clip, talk to me," Harmon voiced over the comms to the defensive bridge.

"Clip!" Harmon said, a little louder.

"He is trying to save the lieutenant commander," a translated voice said.

Harmon bolted from the commander's chair for the lift, hoping it would work. *No! Not Jayneen*, he thought. He began running to the DB.

When Harmon arrived at the DB, he saw Clip at a smoking console. There was a chemical extinguisher lying beside him. He had Jayneen's cube out on the console. One corner was blackened, and he was frantically trying to attach his music box, slate, and a power cell to it.

"Squat!" Clip kept shouting over and over as he worked. His fingers were a blur, and after about five minutes, he sat back, clearly exhausted.

"Is she…" Harmon asked quietly.

"I don't know, man…I just don't know," Clip said, running his hand through his hair.

"My music box has the largest hard drive I have available. Frost! It was the only one I had available," he said. "I couldn't move her to the ship because of the power surges. Everything that makes Jayneen…Jayneen, is her core program. The only way to know is to transfer what I have to another one of those." He gestured toward the alien computer.

"Where do we get one of those? Is there another on the ship?" Harmon asked.

"No, it was the only one we had. The only place to get another would be their home system," Clip said.

"How in the frost do we get there? That's one of the gate locations that isn't on the net. Only Jayneen had those," Harmon said, staring at the music box.

"She gave it to us," Clip said, pointing back to his console.

Harmon looked at the screen at Clip's station. A set of coordinates was centered on it. She had sent the coordinates as the console was burning. The screen was flickering.

"Did you record the number? It looks like that station is about to burn up," Harmon said. The fifty-digit number disappeared, then came back on.

"I got it...here," Clip said, pointing at his head. "I'll never forget it."

* * * * *

Chapter Twenty-Eight

alvage Title came within missile range of the heavy
troop carrier *Endless Krill* hours after it had launched
all its dropships. The Squilla had been able to make
several trips back and forth, and the only Squilla occupying the
transport was a skeleton crew. The young officer that had been left
in charge was no fool. He started sending the surrender signal long
before the ship could be engaged. Harmon had him place the ship in
high altitude, and he sent Big Jon with a team to ensure there was no
foul play. There were only eight of the six-foot-tall Squilla on board.
They were locked in a room with a heavily-armed team to guard
them. Clip was able to use his program to lock out the carrier's controls, and a team was also sent to occupy the bridge of the giant ship.

When Staff Sergeant Jontilictick came back into the shuttle and
the bay door was closed again, Harmon held a meeting near the
Hauler. The Squilla had taken the capitol and its surrounding area.
There were two thousand claw soldiers and one hundred of the shell
tanks on the surface. There were also the eight dropships that had
brought them there, which could be used as air support in a limited
fashion.

"Are we sure the Squilla that talked wasn't lying about their
numbers?" Clip asked.

"Oh, I'm sure," Big Jon said. His repair team had lost three
members during the fight to seal the breached decks. He was looking
for some payback.

"Good enough for me," Clip said.

"Ok, here's the plan," Harmon said. "Zerith, you stay here on *Salvage Title*. Clip, you pilot *Hauler* with Big Jon and twenty of his crew. When we get down, we'll meet up with Wilton and his Marines. I'm coming down in the Zax to see what I can do. The Tretrayon ground defense has a few aircraft, but not many. It looks like the Squilla did a number on the airfield in Tretra City where the aircraft were. They also wreaked havoc on the motor pool. Lieutenant General Wilton tells me they only have twelve serviceable tanks, some light artillery, and a total of three hundred mechs with pilots after the bombing runs those dropships made."

"What happened to the fleet's dropships?" Clip asked.

"When the carrier made orbit, it hit the planet with space-to-surface missiles. The ships have been destroyed, and there are just remnants of the ground defense forces left," Harmon answered. "Maybe if the system government hadn't limited it to a division-sized force, we wouldn't be trying to figure out how to dig the Squilla out of the capitol."

* * *

Harmon roared into the planet's atmosphere in the Zax. He wasn't sure what type of defenses the Squilla dropships might have, and he figured speed would help. He flew past what remained of the System Capitol Building and saw where the Squilla had parked the dropships. They were on the back lawn of the capitol. Some of the shell tanks started firing at him as he flew past.

He circled back around and angled for a strafing run. The lasers on the fighter fired, and two of the tanks exploded. He circled back around to make a pass over the dropships.

One of the crews in the dropships was alert, and it started firing its top-mounted turret at Harmon. He jinked back and forth randomly, and, as he flew back over the dropships, he hit the switch on the makeshift bomb bay that Hank and Stan had added to the Zax, and seventy-two thermite grenades came tumbling out. Some grenades landed near the dropships, some landed on them, and many rolled under them.

They started going off, and from what Harmon could see as he circled, they were not as good as thermite—they were much better. They packed an explosive that dispersed a gel compound out in a twenty-foot radius. Wherever the gel landed, it stuck and started burning like the tip of a welder. *Wish I had more of those*, Harmon thought.

"What was in those?" Clip asked over the comms.

"I don't know, but we need more of it," Harmon answered. "How did you see it?"

"I hacked a satellite. I could read a slate in someone's hands sitting in the park. If anyone was out on the streets, that is. It's a government satellite," Clip said. "Not many people know they're up there."

"That's crazy. Are there any over Joth?" Harmon asked.

"Sure, but they always seem to malfunction. Must be the magnetic poles. The system government quit sending them over about six years ago. Go figure," Clip said.

More of the top turrets fired at the Zax, and the ship jumped suddenly as a number of warning lights illuminated on Harmon's instrument panel. "Frost! I'm hit!" he said, struggling with the fighter's controls. "One engine is out, and the fuel level is dropping! I've got to put it down. Come get me."

Harmon landed the Zax about twenty miles away in the huge parking lot of a rundown shopping center. The port engine was still smoking, even after he had hit the emergency extinguishers, but it was no longer on fire.

He climbed down and locked the hatch, hoping nobody would fool around with it. From his time at the academy, Harmon knew the neighborhood he'd landed in was known for gangs and crime. Tretra may have looked beautiful from orbit, but that was only because the government controlled the majority of the land and didn't allow most citizens access to it. In the cities, where the majority of the population was located, it was a different story.

The cities tended to be block after block of government-controlled housing. The rent was free, utilities were free, and for the most part, safety was free; however, there were parts of the capital city where law enforcement refused to go. It was a little better in election years, as more of the budget was spent on social centers and subsidy raises, but some places remained in the hands of the gangs.

The party in power also controlled the system government. Both planets voted, but with a population of almost five hundred million across Tretra, the system president was always the head of the party that controlled Tretra.

The *Hauler* landed just as a group of people were gathering on the other side of the street, and Big Jon came out to make sure Harmon was alright and to see if he needed anything brought over from the Zax. The crowd edged closer.

"You think you're just going to leave that there?" a large bald man asked. One side of his face was tattooed with lightning bolts. The tattoo seemed to shimmer with a life of its own. "Shouldn't you be stopping them crabs?" he asked with contempt.

Harmon looked over and didn't say a word. When he had attended the academy, he had been briefed the first day to stay out of the housing centers. It was best to just move on and keep the peace.

"Hey! I'm talking to you...and that freak with you," the man said, stepping out into the abandoned street.

Staff Sergeant Jontilictick looked over at the man and then back to Harmon. Harmon shook his head slightly. They started walking toward the *Hauler*.

"That's right. Walk away. This whole area belongs to the Bolts! You leave that here and it's ours. We'll scrap it. We'll scrap all of it. You hear me?" he shouted. Several of his tattooed companions encouraged him.

Harmon stopped and turned around. He started to step toward the group when Big Jon put a hand out to stop him. Big Jon took his knife out of its sheath and handed it to Harmon, handle first. He unsnapped his holster, slid his pistol out, and handed it to him as well. Harmon noticed that it was one of Zerith's modified pistols.

The man realized what the Leethog was doing, stepped away from his friends, started rolling his neck and shrugging his shoulders. He appeared ready to teach the alien a lesson. It was obvious he hadn't become the gang's leader by a vote.

Big Jon stepped up to the man who towered over him by more than a foot. The man swung with a hard-right cross...that met air, and then Big Jon beat the man like he had stolen something from him.

Harmon watched the fight in awe. He knew his own fighting abilities, but he had to admit to himself that even he might not want to tangle with that Leethog. It was a fighting style that Harmon was not familiar with. Raw and violent, yet fluid in its movements. Several of the gang members waded in when they realized the direction the fight was going. It was their mistake.

One of the other members who was over to the side slid a projectile pistol out from under his jacket. Harmon fired a laser round between the man's feet, and he dropped the weapon, raised his hands, and eased away from it.

The fight was over, and four men were face down in the street. The gang leader was sitting up, holding the side of his face—it looked like his jaw was fractured. The crowd on the other side of the street had dispersed.

"They will think twice about insulting a Leethog next time," Big Jon said, sliding his knife back into its sheath.

The gang members couldn't understand him without translators. Harmon looked over at the gang and said, "He said if anyone so much as touches that fighter, he will hunt you down and skin the tattoos off of your faces. He has your scent and can track you to the ends of this planet."

At hearing this, Big Jon started laughing. A Leethog hissing with all its teeth exposed wasn't something anyone unfamiliar with the race would ever want to see. There was a look of genuine fear in the gang leader's eyes.

"What the frost was that all about?" Clip asked them when they sat down in the operations center of the *Hauler*.

"Just a little workout before the big fight," Big Jon said nonchalantly.

"Workout? Looks like you beat the squat out of them to me," Clip said, lifting off. "Did you kill anyone?"

"No, I gave the captain my knife," he said, grinning.

* * * * *

Chapter Twenty-Nine

"**H**eard you had a little problem with your fighter," Lieutenant General Wilton said.

He was in the temporary headquarters three miles from the capital. The remainder of the ground defense forces and the Marines from the fleet were holed up in defensive positions on the edge of a huge park, with the trees between them and the Squilla.

"Just a bit, sir," Harmon answered.

"I also heard the reports of the battle with the Squilla task force. Without you and your ship, we wouldn't even be here planning this. The entire system owes a debt to you and your crew that can never be paid," he said.

"Sir, it's my system, too," Harmon said. "We just did what had to be done. Sometimes things work out in your favor. All of us have lost a lot these last few weeks."

"That we did," Wilton said. "None of it would have happened if first fleet hadn't been sent out like mercenaries. It's one thing to do that for a living; there are some good companies out there. But when you go out representing an entire system…trouble is going to follow you home.

"The Squilla had them two-to-one from the beginning," he continued. "It was a slaughter. Speaking of which, the scouts have reported back in on the slaughter here, and will be back in an hour for debriefing. The short story is that our system president, the planetary president, and a majority of the members of all three houses are dead. The Squilla dropped missiles on them when they were in an emergency meeting."

"Wait, that means that President Benter is now the system president," Harmon said, remembering his meeting with the president.

"He is. He is the first system president from Joth. A Prithmar named Chazzig is now president of Joth," the General said.

"President Benter is a good one to have. Vice President Chazzig, too. I voted for both of them last cycle," Harmon said.

"Once we clear the Squilla from the capitol, it's sure going to get interesting. Do you know who the president of Tretra is now?" he asked.

"No, sir; I have no idea. You said most of all three houses were killed. How does the succession run here?" Harmon asked.

"Gerald Bentalt, the Secretary of Agriculture, is next in line. A circuit judge will be swearing him in this afternoon," he said.

"Nice, that's Twiggy's father. He is a good choice," Harmon said.

"There was no choice; it is written in the Constitution. There have been a lot of changes made to it over the years. That is one they never got around to. Something tells me the party that has been in power for so long is on its way out the door. Good riddance to them," Lieutenant General Wilton said. "But you didn't hear me say that. No politics in the fleet and all that."

"Roger that, sir," Harmon said, hiding a smile.

"Who is Twiggy, anyway?" the general asked.

"Lieutenant Bentalt of the ground defensive forces, sir," Harmon answered.

"Is he the tall guy that was in the competition? He's been put on active status and was over by the ammo depot prepping his mech, last I saw," he said. "We only have a few of the GDF mechs and pilots. Just the ones from their reserves. The rest were lost in the missile strikes."

Harmon was relieved to know that Twiggy was still in the fight. He would have to catch up with him later. Right now, he was waiting for Evelyn to come back with the other scouts. There were priorities, after all.

An hour later, Evelyn came into the tent. Her hair was matted from wearing her helmet, but she looked just as beautiful as Harmon had ever seen. She smiled and walked right into his arms. He held her for several minutes before they broke apart, and he kissed her. The regulations could dive into a sand pit for all he cared. Besides, he wasn't actually *in* the fleet.

"Ahem. If you two are done, we have a planning session to start," Lieutenant General Wilton said, though he was smiling as he said it. They let go and took a seat at the table. Several others were already seated.

Around the table with Harmon and Evelyn were Clip, Lieutenant General Wilton, Twiggy, and Major Audell. Twiggy was the highest-ranking member of the ground defense forces left. Major Audell, who Harmon remembered from the Best Marine Competition, was the highest-ranking mech pilot.

"The Squilla have set up a perimeter around the capitol grounds. We don't know why, since most of it is one big crater, but that is where they are. From the looks of things, they plan on being there for some time. They have shell tanks dug in and covering all avenues of approach. We counted fifty defilades. The only things showing are the barrels of their guns," Lieutenant Stacey said.

The Squilla shell tank was a small tank operated by one occupant. It was shaped like a seashell with a low silhouette, and its main gun was a powerful laser. They had to be recharged every three or four days, and the scouts had identified several charging vehicles that were fusion-powered. All of the tanks were expected to be close to fully charged since they had only been planet-side for half a day.

"Can't do much about those unless we hit 'em from above. Any missiles left in that carrier?" Twiggy asked.

"No, they used all they had before they came down," Clip answered. "I pulled up the ordnance inventory and checked. The missiles we have left on *Salvage Title* won't work either—they have the wrong kind of guidance system. Given enough time, I could program some."

"We don't have time. The sooner we clear the planet of invaders, the better. It will send a message back to their king that he needs to find some other system to invade," said Admiral Timerton, who was present through a video call relay.

Harmon agreed. They needed to end this quickly. Then he could start planning a trip to Jayneen's home system to see if she could be saved. He wasn't sure what the long-term solution might be for this whole mess, but it was something they could worry about later.

"I have an idea. We could send in a team to plant explosives on a section of the dug-in tanks and then bring the mechs in through the hole in their defenses. Once we have taken care of the tanks, we could worry about their soldiers," Harmon suggested.

"That would work, but the timing has to be right. We have to hit the hole before they can roll up any backup tanks. They currently have fifty in the ground; that leaves a little over fifty available to them," Lieutenant General Wilton said. "We can't get in a prolonged battle with them. We are severely limited on charging stations for the mechs. Our dropships are junk, and they hit the Yatarward Industries facilities in their preparatory bombardment. There's not much left there to help us."

"We have two mobile chargers that the scouts use, and now your charger in *Hauler*," said Major Audell.

"There are two chargers in *Hauler*'s ready room. We could run some lines and extend the plugs into the bay," Harmon said.

"Two? You have two mechs?" Major Audell asked.

"No, I have two power cells in the mech," Harmon answered, grinning.

"No wonder that thing dominated," Major Audell said.

"It helps. However, in the end, it's going to come down to old-fashioned infantry tactics," stated Twiggy. "They have two thousand troops, and we don't have nearly as many. Even if we add in local law enforcement, we might end up with a thousand bodies. Two-to-one is not the kind of odds we want to face against an enemy with natural armor. Unless you hit one of 'em just right, they can shrug off most handheld laser weapons. Their exoskeletons reflect the blasts."

"As long as we have the use of mechs, we should be able to lower the numbers," Harmon said.

"True, but once their power cells run down, we are on our own two legs armed with what we can carry," Evelyn remarked.

"If we can get that platoon of tanks in, it can surely help support the infantry," said Twiggy.

"What if we use the artillery we have in conjunction with our tanks on the opposite side of their perimeter, and we hit it as a distraction?" Harmon suggested. "We can keep them occupied that way and then hit them from this side. If we keep the *Hauler* out at its maximum range, we can use it as part of the distraction, too. We just need to make sure it stays out of range, though, because it doesn't have military shielding, and it is not the most maneuverable thing to fly."

"Yeah, not being shot would be cool with me," Clip agreed.

"Sounds like we have the workings of a plan," Lieutenant General Wilton said. "How are we going to get anyone close enough to set charges without being picked up on their sensors? Any type of night optics or electronics will give them away."

"I have it covered, sir. Trust me," Harmon said.

Harmon walked out and noticed a couple people waiting on him. One was Marteen Yatarward. Curious, Harmon walked over.

"What's up?" he asked.

"Harmon, I've been an ass. At the academy, hell...all my life. When I found out...when I found out that my whole family had been killed in the missile attacks, I sat down and just thought. I realized credit, the company, and my name wasn't worth squat when it comes down to it. What matters is the people around you and how you treat them. Gunny Harper here has shown me that if you respect people and treat them fairly, they'll do the same to you. Back during the competition, I backslid a little. Hell, even then I wasn't the guy you knew in school. Gunny let me know it after the competition, too. He was right, as usual," Marteen said. "I have already apologized to Evelyn. I wanted to apologize to you, too."

Harmon took his outstretched hand and looked into Marteen's eyes. He meant his apology; Harmon could accept it.

"Fresh slate," Harmon said, smiling.

Harmon reached out to shake the gunnery sergeant's hand, as well. It dawned on him that he recognized the man; he had fought him in the competition.

"Let me apologize for the ol' one-two I gave you, Gunny," Harmon said.

"Hey, sir; no apology needed. Even a crusty old Marine like myself can still learn. That was a hell of thing. You have to teach that maneuver to me some time," Gunnery Sergeant Harper said.

That night, Big Jon and the twenty Leethog in his crew prepared to move out. They had satchels full of explosives with remote detonators, and were going to go in on the east side of the perimeter and set charges on ten of the Squilla tanks. They didn't need any type of light enhancement; starlight provided more than enough for them. Since both moons were half full, it was like the middle of the day for them.

"Get in, set the charges, and get out. We need to blow them up just as daylight is breaking," Harmon said. "Twenty of us will drop from the *Hauler* as Clip goes over to the west side for the distraction. He is going to head out to drop off the last of the tanks as soon as they are loaded," Harmon said.

"In and out like the Charquin, I got it," Big Jon said.

"Right. What's a Charquin?" Harmon asked.

"She is the one who steals little ones in the night when they misbehave," the Leethog replied. "They never see their families again."

"What the frost? Remind me to never get a bedtime story from a Leethog," Clip said as he walked to the *Hauler*.

* * * * *

Chapter Thirty

Big Jon and his team of Leethog infiltrators split up within sight of the Capitol Center. From the tree line on the edge of the park, Big Jon could make out the tank positions. His team leaders had their instructions; it would be two to a tank. Big Jon opted to go with the youngest Leethog in the platoon. She was a little nervous, but she hid it well. From this point on, they would all communicate by hand and ear signals. He had decided that they would go in without gear to cut down on noise. Their gear was waiting for them twenty yards back in the trees and around the base of a towering oak, planted hundreds of years ago on Colony Day.

Staff Sergeant Jontilictick and Private Jesstilgalton dropped to all fours and low crawled for two hundred meters. Big Jon looked from left to right and could barely see flashes of movement as his crew inched their way to the perimeter. Even his sensitive ears could detect very little noise from their passing. As they approached their assigned tank, he could see there was a problem.

Jess saw it, too. She signaled to him with waving ears. She raised first one, then the other, then both at once. Trouble. Big Jon indicated he understood with his left hand. He signaled to her to stay back as he eased forward.

The top half of the tank he had selected, just above the barrel, was open all the way back. Its occupant was not inside. He eased around the tank and saw the Squilla. By the way it kept raising and straightening its legs one at a time, it appeared as if it had exited the tank to stretch. If it decided to move around, there was a chance it might notice one of the team members placing charges. The Squilla would have to be taken out if it didn't get back into the tank.

Big Jon eased back and signaled for Jess to place the charges under the front of the barrel where the turret rotated. He pulled his knife and waited in the shadows. Jess placed the charges quickly and set the fuse. It was below the barrel, in its shadow, and couldn't be seen. She eased down and disappeared into the dark in front of the tank where she waited for the staff sergeant. The Squilla climbed up on the tank to get back in but hesitated, looking over to the next tank in line.

The Squilla raised up to get a better look; it had seen something. Big Jon couldn't take any chances. In a flash, he was up on the front of the tank, he sank his knife into the soft slot where one of the Squilla's eyestalks met its shell. He pulled the knife out and stabbed it deep below the other eyestalk. The Squilla never made a sound. Its legs went straight, it started convulsing, and it dropped into the tank with some of its legs sticking out above it. Big Jon stuffed the legs into the tank and shut the hatch. It was heavy, and it took everything he had to do it, but he got it closed. He stayed low, wiped his blade, and sheathed his knife. It was time to head back to the woods.

They all met back at the tree and put their gear on. The Leethog troops all had combat gear: light armor, helmets with comms, and ammo harnesses. All of them had pistols and rifles from the ready room on the *Hauler*. Zerith, Hank, and Stan had modified all of them during their transits. It had given the brothers something to do that Zerith could supervise. Each Leethog had five of the fragmentation grenades, too.

Big Jon had opted to use one of the magnetic propulsion rifles. It was similar to a railgun and launched a metal pellet at an incredible velocity. Zerith was pretty sure it would penetrate a Squilla's body. The staff sergeant had a laser pistol strapped to his hip, as well. He was the only Leethog wearing different gear—the heavy battle armor that had been found when the weapons were discovered. Since he was over five feet tall, it fit him. It had comms, a full charge for its helmet, and the servo-assisted skeleton built in.

The artillery barrage started just moments after the system's star broke over the horizon. Moments later, the tanks started firing from their maximum range. The *Hauler*'s turrets fired on the Squilla positions on the west side of the perimeter, as well. After two salvos, the artillery stopped firing.

Tanks on the east side blew apart, and the twenty mechs dropped inside the perimeter. Several minutes later, Major Audell led two hundred and eighty mechs through the gap, firing their railguns at the tanks on the left and right as they advanced.

It was not without cost. The Squilla tank's main gun was a powerful laser that took off limbs when striking a mech, although the Marines and GDF forces piloting the mechs continued to fight if they were able. Harmon saw several mechs firing their railguns even though their other arm was missing. A few were forced to eject and use their grenade rifles.

* * *

Harmon had done his best to even out the odds during the drop, firing missiles into the hatches of several tanks as he fell. Several of the tanks were taken out before they ever fired a shot. Although the tanks were not as mobile as the mechs, they were still tanks, and they put up a frost of a fight.

Harmon saw the Leethog come through the gap with around fifty of the GDF soldiers. They spread out into teams of four and began moving toward the capitol building, picking off the Squilla soldiers near the building who were firing at the mechs with tripod-mounted lasers. The mechs were busy with the tanks, and the crew-served lasers had taken several of the mechs out. Harmon saw the heavy battle armor with the two extra arms, locked tight against the chest in front, several times during the battle. He knew it had to be Big Jon.

Harmon felt his mech get knocked sideways, and he fought to stay upright. An empty missile rack had been burnt off by a laser blast from a tank. Harmon did a rocket-assisted jump and leaped up on top of the tank, and he fired his railgun at another tank on the far side of a crater. While he was firing, he brought his left arm down with the cutting laser that Zerith had attached burning at full power. There was more than one way to get to the tank's occupant.

Harmon fired his leg thrusters and flew above another one of the tanks that was maneuvering through the wreckage. The tank he left behind was a smoking wreck. The laser had burned through the hatch, and he had kept at it for a full thirty seconds after that. He landed and started the laser again.

The battle lasted for several hours. After the first few frantic minutes, the Squilla tanks in reserve quit trying to maneuver out to the perimeter and had used the devastated terrain to their advantage to take long shots at the mechs. In the end, the last few tanks and some Squilla infantry had used the rubble from destroyed buildings as cover, and they had held the few mechs with ammunition at bay.

Harmon was out of rocket fuel and couldn't come over the top of them. Big Jon and several members of his team had gotten close enough to take out the soldiers and throw satchel charges underneath the last three tanks. They had succeeded, but Big Jon lost two Leethog in the attempt.

With the heavy forces destroyed, the only thing left to do was clear the Squilla soldiers from the rest of the capitol buildings and the city beyond. It was not going to be an easy task. There were over eighteen hundred still holed up in the buildings.

* * *

N'Tikah, the Squilla shell commander, had W'Coltah taken out of his sight and locked up—the coward had suggested surrendering to the humans. *I should have pried his shell open in front of the claw soldiers while he screamed*, he thought. That was the problem with the members of the Squilla Navy. They could not fight without their ships around them. *N'Tikah and his claw soldiers would hold out until the king sent reinforcements, period.*

N'Tikah had ordered his personal aide to ensure the human carcasses were divided among the companies so his claw soldiers could eat. It would hold them for several days before they needed to gather more food. They had found some humans cowering in the basement of one of the large buildings of the system's capital. The ones who hadn't died in the missile barrage did so as soon as they were found hiding. He had them cut up like chum.

He couldn't believe the humans of this world had such a small military, and that it had been so easily wiped out by the initial missile bombardment. He would have thought the beings inhabiting the world would have risen up to fight the invaders, but he had seen no sign of it. The local video services kept repeating over and over for them to seek shelter. It was ridiculous. If any race ever landed on Squill, the Squilla would rise from all of the seas to fight, even without weapons. They would defend the females and the young. *Ridiculous.*

He heard the artillery rounds exploding as his aide came scuttling into the command center to tell him the second company commander had detected movement of enemy tanks to the west. The sound of rounds impacting inside the perimeter, as well as explosions on the front of the dug-in positions, told him the humans had finally decided to fight back. *Good*, he thought. *We will finish this.*

N'Tikah ordered reinforcements on that side, and twenty-five more tanks rolled into position between the dug-in ones. Moments later, he realized his mistake; at least ten tanks on the east side blew apart. It appeared as if charges had been set on them. The idiots in third company had allowed infiltrators to get close to them during the night. *He would have that commander's shell split*, he thought. He ordered the remainder of his tanks to the east side, and they began maneuvering around the craters and destroyed buildings. Then twenty mechs dropped among the tanks and started firing missiles and railguns.

"Send out fourth and fifth companies to support the shell tanks," N'Tikah ordered over the comms. "Have them use the crew-served lasers. Destroy those machines."

The cursed humans had deployed their bipedal mechs. *They had to build shells to protect their weak bodies*, he thought. The information they had on them was that they were mobile but limited in armament. Once the humans were depleted of their rounds, they would have to be reloaded. If the Squilla could hold out until then, they could defeat the humans. He couldn't believe they had so many mechs—he'd thought the preparatory bombardment had taken out the factory where they were made as well as most of the ground forces on the planet.

N'Tikah watched through the video feeds of several different shell tanks as the battle was fought. He noticed a particularly large mech that seemed to be all over the place. It was knocked sideways as a tank's laser blasted a missile rack off its shoulder. After this, it leapt onto a shell tank, fired a continuous laser into the hatch, and shot kinetic projectiles at another tank across a crater. Whoever piloted that machine had no fear.

A heavy weapons team started to set up the tripod of a crew-served laser. They would have a clear shot of that mech's back. *Yes*, he thought. Out of nowhere, a smaller being climbed onto the rear of a burning tank, ran across the top, and jumped a considerable distance to land on the gunner's back. N'Tikah saw a glint of silver as the arm slammed down into a claw soldier's shell over and over. Before its teammate could react, the soldier fired a rifle several times between its eyestalks. *Even their infantry had shells built for them*, he thought.

Hours later, N'Tikah gathered with the remaining company commanders. There were only sixteen Squilla companies and the headquarters company left—only eighteen hundred Squilla remained to face whatever the humans threw at them. He ordered his commanders to have each of their companies separate into ten squads. "Hide along the buildings of this city. Destroy what you can. Eat when you must. Make your way to the coast. We will regroup offshore and wait for reinforcements. We have all been out of water too long," he said.

"They will not hunt us in the seas?" the fourteenth company commander asked. It was an honest question. N'Tikah knew him well; E'Marik was no coward.

"This race cannot survive in the sea. They are air breathers. We will be safe," N'Tikah said.

* * * * *

Chapter Thirty-One

Harmon fell backward into a chair in the command tent, exhausted. All the beings that participated in the attack were just as exhausted. The adrenaline rush and its following crash took a toll on a being. Not to mention the energy expended while fighting. He was tired, but he had to know the outcome.

"How bad was it, sir?" he asked.

"We lost one hundred and ninety-two mech pilots, seven men from the tank crews, twenty-eight GDF, and eight Leethog. Two tanks were destroyed in addition to two hundred and nine mechs. We are out of railgun rounds and mech missiles. On the positive side, we have around five hundred law enforcement and armed farmers gathered ten miles from here. We would have more, but most law enforcement personnel just have stun guns issued to them. We are trying to get the logistics together on that. How many weapons, what type, rounds…that sort of thing. I'm putting Lieutenant Bentalt in charge of that group. He'll have to pick some subordinates from law enforcement, but that should be simple since they have leadership in place. Mostly," Lieutenant General Wilton said.

"Twiggy can handle it, sir," Harmon said, dismayed at the loss of life.

"I hate to lose him as a mech pilot, but he had his mech shot out from under him. It's a wonder the laser didn't kill him. The blast blew the whole side of his mech out. He is so skinny he walked away with only first-degree burns on his side," he said. "If we had any more mechs, I would climb back into one myself, even though it's been years," he added, frustrated.

"Can we get any help from other cities here or from other continents?" Harmon asked.

"Not going to happen. That Squilla carrier orbited several times as it prepped the planet. Every major airfield, every space port, and even the shipbuilding facilities in orbit were hit," Wilton answered.

"No wonder there are no missiles left on the carrier," Harmon said.

"Sir, my people tell me that the Squilla have started moving through the city. They appear to be heading toward the coast. If they get to the water, we won't be able to hunt them down," Evelyn said. She had been sitting with her head down, resting. Harmon had thought she was asleep.

"I know. On their planet, they live both in and out of the seas," Lieutenant General Wilton said, frustrated. "I don't know that we can stop them."

"We've got to do something," Harmon said.

* * *

Nobody noticed Clip ease out of the tent. He had a plan. He walked into the bay of the *Hauler* and went up to the operations center. Big Jon was sitting there, sharpening his knife.

"I heard you lost some," Clip said, as he sat down.

"I did. They knew it was a possibility when we hired them back home. We all did. It doesn't make it any easier, though," he said, testing the knife's edge.

"Well, I'm about to make a call, and I'm probably going to be jumping over every bit of command to do it. You in?" Clip asked, looking over sideways at the staff sergeant.

"Will it help me get some revenge?" Big Jon asked.

"Oh, yeah. If it works out the way I think it will, the Squilla will never even smell the sea on Tretra." Clip said.

"Make the call," Big Jon said as he slid his knife into its sheath.

* * *

"Sir, you have a call on sscreen," the new Tretrayon System President's personal assistant said.

"Who is it?" President Benter asked. "And how did they get this comm address? It's brand new,"

"He ssayss his name iss Clip," she said.

"Well, if he has this address and asked for me, he must be important. Put him on screen," he said.

A young man appeared on the screen. President Benter didn't recognize him. He appeared to be calling from a small ship's bridge.

"Can I help you?" the president questioned.

"You know it," Clip said. "Check it out…"

* * * * *

Chapter Thirty-Two

Harmon woke up late the next morning and walked outside of the *Hauler*. He heard ships, and then he looked up and saw them. Ships of all shapes and sizes were coming into the atmosphere and looked to be landing at the beach fifty miles away. There were small ships coming in, larger ones that were just a little smaller than the *Hauler*, and two that Harmon knew belonged to companies in the moisture retention business that took the exports to other systems.

Harmon wondered what they were doing. He also wondered why he hadn't been awakened by anyone that morning. They needed to figure out a way to stop the Squilla from making their way to the sea with the limited resources and beings they had.

He walked into the tent and was surprised to see two Prithmar, a Yalteen, a Caldivar, and two men that, judging by their clothes, were obviously from Joth. The beings were all seated around a table with Lieutenant General Wilton. Harmon's chair was empty, so he took a seat.

"Nice of you to join us today," the Yalteen said through a translator.

Harmon recognized him; they'd been friends since secondary school. "Mahnoot!" Harmon exclaimed. "What are you doing here? Shouldn't you be running the grappler?"

"Rinto gave me some time off. Thank you for the good word to him, by the way," the big Yalteen answered.

"What's this all about, sir?" Harmon asked.

"It appears somebody we know called the system president directly on a private link and told him he had an idea," Lieutenant General Wilton said.

"Clip," Harmon said, without hesitation.

"You guessed it. So now what we have are an armed Joth militia of fifty-five hundred members and rising. It looks like by the end of the day, we will have over ten thousand members. More in the next few days if we need them. The system and planet president declared martial law on Tretra and did away with the personal weapons ban. Then they called Joth's new president for a favor. He requested volunteers from the Joth militia," Lieutenant General Wilton said.

The Joth militia was the unofficial military on the planet Joth. The planet had no real military, as the system government had designated the ground defense force to be sufficient for both planets. However, none of the GDF was stationed on Joth.

Even though the system government had tried numerous times to enact a personal weapons ban on Joth, it had never even been close. There were more weapons than beings on Joth. The militia met every other month at various times, depending on the community's needs. It was never official, yet it always *was*.

The militia drilled for an entire weekend. Physical training, combatives, weapons training, target practice, communications, and calls for fire were part of the weekend. All over Joth, there were garages with armored hovercraft parked in the back. There were modified construction equipment vehicles with cannons. In the last month or so, some beings had even been building mechs.

Many companies on Joth had removable turrets on their small spacecraft. There were rumors that some of the Farnog Corporate ships could defend themselves should they be attacked by pirates. Companies and businesses on both poles looked the other way when employees asked for certain weekends off.

The word had gone out that their sister planet needed help. The beings of Joth had not hesitated to help, despite having been treated as second class by the humans on Tretra. When a neighbor needed you, you came. It didn't matter if your families had a running dispute for years. When the sand blows in, you go, shovel in hand and containers of water in the back of your hovercraft.

Clip is a genius, Harmon thought. *For real.* There was no way a single Squilla was going to make it to the sea. Things were starting to look up.

"Where do you want these?" Harmon heard a voice ask.

He looked up, and there was Rinto, carrying what appeared to be a heavy box in his mechanical arm. Rinto had an entire box of mech charging plugs. There were at least thirty plugs in the box.

"I have been collecting these things for years. Most of them will fit the new mechs, I think. Ya got anybody that can wire them up? I brought a portable fusion plant. I use it to charge the grappler," Rinto said. "Oh, and there are cases of railgun rounds in the cargo hold. I ain't lifting those. The fine beings at the railgun plant on Joth donated them."

* * * * *

Chapter Thirty-Three

Two months later, Evelyn watched as Harmon directed operations on the bridge of *Salvage Title*. Zerith and the repair crews, with help from what was left of the ship-building facility, had fixed its fusion plant and engines. All of the compartments that had been breached were repaired. It wasn't a pretty job, but it was sufficient. Hank and Stan called it a monster weld. It was big, ugly, and strong.

Harmon had sent video messages to the families of all the crew members who had died. It was one of the hardest things he had ever done. The system president had insisted on the government paying the costs to send them through the gate.

The ship had some new crew members. Many former fleet members had signed on to Tomeral and Associates since the Tretrayon fleet now consisted of only a few Tretrayon ships, a Squilla troop carrier, and a couple other Squilla ships. They were assigned throughout the *Salvage Title*.

A handful of Prithmar had signed up to work in engineering. They were experienced with fusion plants and propulsion, and Kyla was glad to have them on the team. They quickly learned to do things her way.

Eight Yalteen had applied to join security and ship repair. Big Jon was running them through their drills. Clip thought it was funny to see the huge, blue Yalteens act nervous as frost around a five-foot-four Leethog.

Down in the bay, Hank and Stan were repairing three Zax III's. The museum had donated two more as well as some parts. Twiggy was right there with them. He had to resign from the GDF since his father was the planet president. Favoritism and all that. He figured if he was going to fly a Zax, he needed to know how to repair it. He wasn't worried so much about his own ship as he was the one they were rebuilding for JoJo. Hank and Stan were teaching Twiggy the words for a song that Vera and Kyla would never approve of while they worked. Twiggy kept a grin on his face as much as the brothers did. None of it rhymed when translated, but it was hilarious.

The rest of the bay was covered in shuttles and small craft of all kinds. They were the temporary quarters for one hundred extra crew members. They were rotating through their respective departments daily, learning what they could.

On the bridge, Evelyn sat by JoJo as they headed out to the gate. She was amazed at the confidence Harmon showed as he handled everything. He was coordinating training, checking the status on the different sections on the ship, and directing the two ships attached. It was something that should have taken tens of years.

"TDF *United*. This is *Salvage Title*. Take it easy when you attach. Don't scratch her paint, and don't squish the *Hauler*," Harmon said over the comms to the former vacation cruise ship. The Tretrayon system had purchased it through the net. It had two thousand beings on board; there were humans from both Joth and Tretra on it. There were also Leethog, several other races from Joth, and a few other races from neighboring systems that had heard jobs were available from family members. All of them had experience.

"Hey man, I got this," Clip said from the view screen. "And I'm coming back over there when we arrive and detach. I'm only here for the swimming pools. Who would have thought someone would waste so much water? I'm on a ship of fools. Oh, and Zee says you're missing out on a killer salad bar on the buffet. They have dill pickles. Real ones."

# # # # #

About the Author

Kevin Steverson is a retired veteran of the U.S. Army. He is a published songwriter as well as an author. He lives in the northeast Georgia foothills where he continues to refuse to shave ever again. Trim...maybe. Shave...never! When he is not on the road as a Tour Manager he can be found at home writing in one fashion or another.

* * * * *

The following is an
Excerpt from Book One of In Revolution Born:

The Mutineer's Daughter

Chris Kennedy & Thomas A. Mays

Available Now from Theogony Books

eBook, Paperback, and Audio Book

Excerpt from "The Mutineer's Daughter:"

Kenny dozed at his console again.

There he sat—as brazen as ever—strapped down, suited up, jacked in…and completely checked out. One might make allowances for an overworked man falling asleep during a dull routine, watching gauges that didn't move or indicators that rarely indicated anything of consequence, perhaps even during a quiet moment during their ship's long, long deployment.

But Fire Control Tech Third Class Ken Burnside was doing it— yet again—while the ship stood at General Quarters, in an unfriendly star system, while other parts of the fleet engaged the forces of the Terran Union.

Chief Warrant Officer Grade 2 (Combat Systems) Benjamin "Benno" Sanchez shook his helmeted head and narrowed his eyes at the sailor strapped in to his right. He had spoken to the young weapons engineer a number of times before, through countless drills and mock skirmishes, but the youthful idiot never retained the lesson for long.

"Benno, Bosso," Kenny would plead, "you shouldn't yell at me. You should have me teach others my wisdom!"

Benno would invariably frown and give his unflattering opinion of Kenny's wisdom.

"Get it, ya?" Kenny would reply. "I'm a math guy. Probability, right Warrant? The *Puller's* just a little ship, on the edge of the formation. We scan, we snipe, we mop up, we patrol. We don't go in the middle, tube's blazing, ya? We no tussle with the big Terrans, ya? No damage! No battle! So, something goes wrong, back-ups kick in, buzzer goes off, we mark for fix later. And when's the only time you or the officers don't let a man walk 'round and don't ask for this, don't ask for that? When's the only time a man can catch up on the z's, eh? One and the same time! So I doze. Buzzer goes off, I wake, make a note, doze again till I can work, ya? Such wisdom!"

Benno usually lectured him about complacency. He asked what would happen if they *were* hit, if the shot was hot enough, deep enough, destructive enough to burn through the backup of the backup of the backup. What if they did have to face the Great Test, to rise and work and save the *Puller* themselves?

Kenny would always smile, relieved. "Well, then I be dead, ya? No more maintenance either way. Good enough reason to doze right there!"

Benno could have reported him any number of times, but he never had. Putting it on paper and sending it above them was a two-edged sword. It would solve Kenny's sleepy disdain for order, of that Benno had no doubt, but he also knew he would lose Kenny's trust and the vigorous drive the young ALS plebeian applied to every other task. Plus, it would signal to the officers above that Benno couldn't handle a minor discipline problem on his own. And it would indicate to the ranks below that Benno was no longer one of their own—when he had gone from Chief to Chief Warrant Officer, he had changed his ties, forever.

So Benno growled, but he let it slide, content only he would know about Kenny's acts of passive rebellion. No one else would ever know why the young tech kept getting extra punishment duties. Besides, it wasn't as if Kenny was actually *wrong*, in the fullness of things.

Then, before Benno could check his own side of the console to verify whether things were indeed alright, his internal debate was blown away by the unforgiving, indiscriminate lance of an x-ray laser blast.

The single beam struck the *Puller* a glancing blow, centered on a space just beneath the outer hull and aimed outboard. Armor plate, radiation shielding, piping, wireways, conduit, decking, internal honeycombed structure, atmosphere, and people all ionized and ablated into a dense, mixed plasma. This plasma exploded outward, crushing the spaces surrounding the hit and dealing further physical and thermal damage. Combat Systems Maintenance Central, or CSMC, lay deep within the *Puller's* battle hull—three spaces inward from where the x-ray laser struck—but that meant little next to the awesome destructive power of a Dauphine capital-class xaser warhead.

The forward and port bulkheads in front of them flashed white hot with near-instantaneous thermal energy transfer and peeled away, blown out by the twin shocks of the outward-expanding plasma and the snapping counterforce of explosive decompression. The double blast battered Benno in his seat and threw him against his straps to the left. As the bulkheads vanished, their departure also carried away the CSMC monitoring console the two watch standers shared with them into the black, along with Kenny's seat, and Ken Burnside, himself.

The young engineer disappeared in an instant, lost without ever waking. Benno stared, dumbfounded, at the blank spot where he had been, and of all the possible panicked thoughts that could have come to him, only one rose to the forefront:

Does this validate Kenny's wisdom?

Benno shook his head, dazed and in shock, knowing he had to engage his brain. Looking beyond, he could see the glowing edges of bulkheads and decks gouged out by the fast, hot knife of the nuclear-pumped xaser. Only vaguely could he recall the sudden buffeting of explosive decompression that had nearly wrenched him through the straps of his acceleration couch.

He knew he had things to do. He had to check his suit's integrity. Was he leaking? Was he injured? And what about Kenny? Was he gone, unrecoverable? Or was he waiting for his poor, shocked-stupid boss Benno to reach out and save him?

And there was something else, something important he needed to be doing. He wasn't supposed to just sit here and think of himself or unlucky, lazy Kenny. *Oh no*, thought Benno, still trying to marshal his thoughts back together, *Mio is going to be so angry with me, sitting here like a fool...*

"CSMC, report!"

Benno shook his head against the ringing he hadn't realized filled his ears. He reached out for the comms key on his console, swore at how futile that was, then keyed his suit mic. "Last station calling, this is CSMC. We've taken a hit. I lost my technician, console is...down, hard. Over."

"CSMC, TAO," the *Puller's* Tactical Action Officer said through the suit channel, "pull it together! We just had a near miss by a capital class Dauphine warhead. The battle with the Terrans has spread out of the main body. I have missiles up but zero point-defense. I need guns and beams back, *now!*"

* * * * *

Get "The Mutineer's Daughter" now at:
https://www.amazon.com/dp/B07BRTDBCJ

Find out more about Thomas A. Mays and "In Revolution Born" at:
https://chriskennedypublishing.com

* * * * *

The following is an

Excerpt from Book One of the Earth Song Cycle:

Overture

Mark Wandrey

Now Available from Theogony Books

eBook and Paperback

Excerpt from "Overture:"

Dawn was still an hour away as Mindy Channely opened the roof access and stared in surprise at the crowd already assembled there. "Authorized Personnel Only" was printed in bold red letters on the door through which she and her husband, Jake, slipped onto the wide roof.

A few people standing nearby took notice of their arrival. Most had no reaction, a few nodded, and a couple waved tentatively. Mindy looked over the skyline of Portland and instinctively oriented herself before glancing to the east. The sky had an unnatural glow that had been growing steadily for hours, and as they watched, scintillating streamers of blue, white, and green radiated over the mountains like a strange, concentrated aurora borealis.

"You almost missed it," one man said. She let the door close, but saw someone had left a brick to keep it from closing completely. Mindy turned and saw the man who had spoken wore a security guard uniform. The easy access to the building made more sense.

"Ain't no one missin' this!" a drunk man slurred.

"We figured most people fled to the hills over the past week," Jake replied.

"I guess we were wrong," Mindy said.

"Might as well enjoy the show," the guard said and offered them a huge, hand-rolled cigarette that didn't smell like tobacco. She waved it off, and the two men shrugged before taking a puff.

"Here it comes!" someone yelled. Mindy looked to the east. There was a bright light coming over the Cascade Mountains, so intense it was like looking at a welder's torch. Asteroid LM-245 hit the atmosphere at over 300 miles per second. It seemed to move faster and faster, from east to west, and the people lifted their hands

273

to shield their eyes from the blinding light. It looked like a blazing comet or a science fiction laser blast.

"Maybe it will just pass over," someone said in a voice full of hope.

Mindy shook her head. She'd studied the asteroid's track many times.

In a matter of a few seconds, it shot by and fell toward the western horizon, disappearing below the mountains between Portland and the ocean. Out of view of the city, it slammed into the ocean.

The impact was unimaginable. The air around the hypersonic projectile turned to superheated plasma, creating a shockwave that generated 10 times the energy of the largest nuclear weapon ever detonated as it hit the ocean's surface.

The kinetic energy was more than 1,000 megatons; however, the object didn't slow as it flashed through a half mile of ocean and into the sea bed, then into the mantel, and beyond.

On the surface, the blast effect appeared as a thermal flash brighter than the sun. Everyone on the rooftop watched with wide-eyed terror as the Tualatin Mountains between Portland and the Pacific Ocean were outlined in blinding light. As the light began to dissipate, the outline of the mountains blurred as a dense bank of smoke climbed from the western range.

The flash had incinerated everything on the other side.

The physical blast, travelling much faster than any normal atmospheric shockwave, hit the mountains and tore them from the bedrock, adding them to the rolling wave of destruction traveling east at several thousand miles per hour. The people on the rooftops of Portland only had two seconds before the entire city was wiped away.

Ten seconds later, the asteroid reached the core of the planet, and another dozen seconds after that, the Earth's fate was sealed.

* * * * *

Get "Overture" now at:
https://www.amazon.com/dp/B077YMLRHM/

Find out more about Mark Wandrey and the Earth Song Cycle at:
https://chriskennedypublishing.com/

* * * * *

The following is an

Excerpt from Book One of The Psyche of War:

Minds of Men

Kacey Ezell

Available from Theogony Books

eBook, Paperback, and Audio

Excerpt from "Minds of Men:"

"Look sharp, everyone," Carl said after a while. Evelyn couldn't have said whether they'd been droning for minutes or hours in the cold, dense white of the cloud cover. "We should be overhead the French coast in about thirty seconds."

The men all reacted to this announcement with varying degrees of excitement and terror. Sean got up from his seat and came back to her, holding an awkward looking arrangement of fabric and straps.

Put this on, he thought to her. *It's your flak jacket. And your parachute is just there*, he said, pointing. *If the captain gives the order to bail out, you go, clip this piece into your 'chute, and jump out the biggest hole you can find. Do you understand? You do, don't you. This psychic thing certainly makes explaining things easier*, he finished with a grin.

Evelyn gave him what she hoped was a brave smile and took the flak jacket from him. It was deceptively heavy, and she struggled a bit with getting it on. Sean gave her a smile and a thumbs up, and then headed back to his station.

The other men were checking in and charging their weapons. A short time later, Evelyn saw through Rico's eyes as the tail gunner watched their fighter escort waggle their wings at the formation and depart. They didn't have the long-range fuel capability to continue all the way to the target.

Someday, that long-range fighter escort we were promised will materialize, Carl thought. His mind felt determinedly positive, like he was trying to be strong for the crew and not let them see his fear. That, of course, was an impossibility, but the crew took it well. After all, they were afraid, too. Especially as the formation had begun its descent to the attack altitude of 20,000 feet. Evelyn became gradually aware of the way the men's collective tension ratcheted up with every hundred feet of descent. They were entering enemy fighter territory.

Yeah, and someday Veronica Lake will...ah. Never mind. Sorry, Evie. That was Les. Evelyn could feel the waist gunner's not-quite-repentant grin. She had to suppress a grin of her own, but Les' irreverence was the perfect tension breaker.

Boys will be boys, she sent, projecting a sense of tolerance. *But real men keep their private lives private.* She added this last with a bit of smug superiority and felt the rest of the crew's appreciative flare of humor at her jab. Even Les laughed, shaking his head. A warmth that had nothing to do with her electric suit enfolded Evelyn, and she started to feel like, maybe, she just might become part of the crew yet.

Fighters! Twelve o'clock high!

The call came from Alice. If she craned her neck to look around Sean's body, Evelyn could just see the terrifying rain of tracer fire coming from the dark, diving silhouette of an enemy fighter. She let the call echo down her own channels and felt her men respond, turning their own weapons to cover *Teacher's Pet's* flanks. Adrenaline surges spiked through all of them, causing Evelyn's heart to race in turn. She took a deep breath and reached out to tie her crew in closer to the Forts around them.

She looked through Sean's eyes as he fired from the top turret, tracking his line of bullets just in front of the attacking aircraft. His mind was oddly calm and terribly focused...as, indeed, they all were. Even young Lieutenant Bob was zeroed in on his task of keeping a tight position and making it that much harder to penetrate the deadly crossing fire of the Flying Fortress.

Fighters! Three o'clock low!

That was Logan in the ball turret. Evelyn felt him as he spun his turret around and began to fire the twin Browning AN/M2 .50 caliber machine guns at the sinister dark shapes rising up to meet them with fire.

Got 'em, Bobby Fritsche replied, from his position in the right waist. He, too, opened up with his own .50 caliber machine gun, tracking the barrel forward of the nose of the fighter formation, in order to "lead" their flight and not shoot behind them.

Evelyn blinked, then hastily relayed the call to the other girls in the formation net. She felt their acknowledgement, though it was almost an absentminded thing as each of the girls were focusing mostly on the communication between the men in their individual crews.

Got you, you Kraut sonofabitch! Logan exulted. Evelyn looked through his eyes and couldn't help but feel a twist of pity for the pilot of the German fighter as he spiraled toward the ground, one wing completely gone. She carefully kept that emotion from Logan, however, as he was concentrating on trying to take out the other three fighters who'd been in the initial attacking wedge. One fell victim to Bobby's relentless fire as he threw out a curtain of lead that couldn't be avoided.

Two back to you, tail, Bobby said, his mind carrying an even calm, devoid of Logan's adrenaline-fueled exultation.

Yup, Rico Martinez answered as he visually acquired the two remaining targets and opened fire. He was aided by fire from the aircraft flying off their right wing, the *Nagging Natasha.* She fired from her left waist and tail, and the two remaining fighters faltered and tumbled through the resulting crossfire. Evelyn watched through Rico's eyes as the ugly black smoke trailed the wreckage down.

Fighters! Twelve high!

Fighters! Two high!

The calls were simultaneous, coming from Sean in his top turret and Les on the left side. Evelyn took a deep breath and did her best to split her attention between the two of them, keeping the net strong and open. Sean and Les opened fire, their respective weapons adding a cacophony of pops to the ever-present thrum of the engines.

Flak! That was Carl, up front. Evelyn felt him take hold of the controls, helping the lieutenant to maintain his position in the formation as the Nazi anti-aircraft guns began to send up 20mm shells that blossomed into dark clouds that pocked the sky. One exploded right in front of *Pretty Cass'* nose. Evelyn felt the bottom drop out of her stomach as the aircraft heaved first up and then down. She held on grimly and passed on the wordless knowledge the pilots had no choice but to fly through the debris and shrapnel that resulted.

In the meantime, the gunners continued their rapid fire response to the enemy fighters' attempt to break up the formation. Evelyn took that knowledge—that the Luftwaffe was trying to isolate one of the Forts, make her vulnerable—and passed it along the looser formation net.

Shit! They got Liberty Belle! Logan called out then, from his view in the ball turret. Evelyn looked through his angry eyes, feeling his sudden spike of despair as they watched the crippled Fort fall back, two of her four engines smoking. Instantly, the enemy fighters swarmed like so many insects, and Evelyn watched as the aircraft yawed over and began to spin down and out of control.

A few agonizing heartbeats later, first one, then three more parachutes fluttered open far below. Evelyn felt Logan's bitter knowledge that there had been six other men on board that aircraft. *Liberty Belle* was one of the few birds flying without a psychic on board, and Evelyn suppressed a small, wicked feeling of relief that she hadn't just lost one of her friends.

Fighters! Twelve o'clock level!

* * * * *

Get "Minds of Men" now at:
https://www.amazon.com/dp/B0778SPKQV

Find out more about Kacey Ezell at:
https://chriskennedypublishing.com/

* * * * *

The following is an
Excerpt from Book One of the Revelations Cycle:

Cartwright's Cavaliers

Mark Wandrey

Available Now from Seventh Seal Press

eBook, Paperback, and Audio Book

Excerpt from "Cartwright's Cavaliers:"

The last two operational tanks were trapped on their chosen path. Faced with destroyed vehicles front and back, they cut sideways to the edge of the dry river bed they'd been moving along and found several large boulders to maneuver around that allowed them to present a hull-down defensive position. Their troopers rallied on that position. It was starting to look like they'd dig in when Phoenix 1 screamed over and strafed them with dual streams of railgun rounds. A split second later, Phoenix 2 followed on a parallel path. Jim was just cheering the air attack when he saw it. The sixth damned tank, and it was a heavy.

"I got that last tank," Jim said over the command net.

"Observe and stand by," Murdock said.

"We'll have these in hand shortly," Buddha agreed, his transmission interspersed with the thudding of his CASPer firing its magnet accelerator. "We can be there in a few minutes."

Jim examined his battlespace. The tank was massive. It had to be one of the fusion-powered beasts he'd read about. Which meant shields and energy weapons. It was heading down the same gap the APC had taken, so it was heading toward Second Squad, and fast.

"Shit," he said.

"Jim," Hargrave said, "we're in position. What are you doing?"

"Leading," Jim said as he jumped out from the rock wall.

* * * * *

Get "Cartwright's Cavaliers" now at:
https://www.amazon.com/dp/B01MRZKM95

287

Find out more about Mark Wandrey and the Four Horsemen Universe at:

https://chriskennedypublishing.com/the-four-horsemen-books/

* * * * *

Made in the USA
Monee, IL
10 July 2023

38942618R00164